**It was a ridicu~~lous~~
man she had on~~ly~~**

Madeleine returned ~~something~~
marvellous but, if I might use your cloakroom
first, I've been travelling since six and feel a bit
of a mess.'

His eyes swept over her in a shrewd, assessing
glance, coming to rest on her boyishly
cut, smooth, thick cap of tawny fair hair.
Amusement flared in them for an instant. 'You
don't look it.' His voice, too, was amused.
'There's not a strand out of place.'

He lifted his hand, and for one wild, pulse-
quickening moment she thought he was going
to smooth her hair...

Margaret O'Neill started scribbling at four and began nursing at twenty. She contracted TB and, when recovered, did her British Tuberculosis Association nursing training before general training at the Royal Portsmouth Hospital. She married, had two children, and with her late husband she owned and managed several nursing homes. Now retired and living in Sussex, she still has many nursing contacts. Her husband would have been delighted to see her books in print.

Recent titles by the same author:

THE PRACTICE WIFE

BY
MARGARET O'NEILL

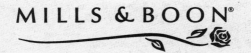

MILLS & BOON®

First published in Great Britain 1998
Harlequin Mills & Boon Limited,
Eton House, 18-24 Paradise Road, Richmond, Surrey TW9 1SR

© Margaret O'Neill 1998

ISBN 0 263 81245 6

Set in Times Roman 10½ on 11¼ pt.
03-9811-52215-D

Printed and bound in Norway
by AiT Trondheim AS, Trondheim

CHAPTER ONE

'YOU'RE mad,' exploded Fee, raising her eyes from the *Nursing Times* and staring at Madeleine. 'Absolutely mad as a hatter.'

Naomi snatched the magazine from Fee's limp fingers and read the ringed advertisement, at first silently and then out loud in an incredulous voice.

'Qualified nurse required for GP practice in Cornwall. Impeccable references essential. Accommodation *may* be available to suitable applicant. Own transport necessary. Salary by negotiation. CV and details to box...'

She, too, stared at Madeleine across the kitchen table littered with the remains of supper. 'And you applied for *this*—when?' She waved the magazine under Madeleine's nose.

'About a week ago.'

'Cornwall! it's out in the sticks, end of the world. What'll you do with yourself when you're not working—what'll you do without us? And a GP practice, for heaven's sake. You'll be bored out of your skull, after battling in Kits' A and E all these years.' She frowned ferociously. 'Why, Maddy, why?'

Madeleine looked at the two faces opposite, loved faces grown familiar over the last ten years. What was she going to do without them? They'd been friends for all that time. They'd started training together, arriving on the same day at St Catherine's—Kits. They'd qualified on the same day, staffed together and taken up sister's posts within weeks of each other. They'd shared a flat until Fee had moved out to marry Tim, her orthopaedic registrar, now poised for a consultancy, and Naomi to live with Brian, a researcher.

Only she, in spite of offers, had remained heart-whole and unattached, living happily alone until recently in this small, comfortable flat which she didn't have to share with anybody.

It hadn't altered the status quo, and their friendship had remained solid. They had a weekly get-together—her turn for supper tonight—and they all still worked at Kits, though Fee was heavily pregnant and would be leaving in a month or so. She and Tim lived only a stone's throw from the hospital, and they would see her frequently. Life would go on much as before.

How could she explain that this was precisely what she couldn't face—an unchanging future, stretching emptily before her? At twenty-seven she both dreaded and longed for change. Not only was she fed up with understaffing, low morale, threatened closures and cutbacks, as were they all, but suddenly her life seemed to have become pointless.

Madeleine felt she was going nowhere, and for the first time ever was unhappy with her work—revolted by it, in fact. She dreaded each day and the endless stream of casualties that passed through her hands, some by accident and some by design—the deliberate infliction of pain by one person on another. She'd seen it all before, coped with it all before, but last week the battered twin babies had been the last straw.

She hadn't been able to speak of it, even to Fee and Naomi. She'd been shaken to the core. She knew that she had to get away from Kits and casualties, from London, crowds and petrol fumes, and breathe some clean, fresh air, slow down the pace of life and take stock of herself. The advertisement had been like an omen, a promise, opening up a new way of life, a new beginning.

'Well?' said Fee impatiently. 'Say something.'

Madeleine took a deep breath. Here goes, she thought... The phone rang. She leapt to her feet and flung open the door to the tiny hall. 'Won't be a minute,' she called over her shoulder, closing the door behind her.

Fee and Naomi made stilted small talk, washed the dishes and made coffee—and tried not to eavesdrop on the muted conversation and long silences coming from the hall.

'Hugo?' wondered Naomi.

'What—from Borneo?'

'Why not? You can phone from anywhere. Perhaps he's missing her, perhaps Maddy's missing him and that's why she's been so down in the dumps lately.'

'But they really were just good friends—and she wasn't broken-hearted when he went off on his medical mission.'

'But he thought a lot of her—bequeathed her Genevieve Two.'

'Only because it's ancient and would only have fetched peanuts on the market.' They grinned at each other. Madeleine's elderly Morris was a joke.

'No, you're right, not Hugo, but who, then? Whoever it is isn't counting the pennies. They've been talking for twenty minutes.'

They turned expectantly as the door from the hall opened and Maddy, looking flushed, stood dramatically in the doorway and said in a hushed voice, 'You'll never guess who that was.' There was an astonished expression in her tawny amber eyes as she glanced from one woman to the other.

Naomi frowned. 'Anyone we know?' she asked.

'Nope.' Madeleine shook her head and, moving slowly across the room, sat at the table.

'Well, tell all,' said Fee briskly, pushing a mug of coffee towards her.

Madeleine wrapped her hands around her mug and stared down into its black depths. 'It was the GP who was advertising for a nurse—a Dr Trellawney.' She took a mouthful of coffee, then raised her head and gave her friends a crooked smile. 'I can't believe it, but he's offered me the job... And...and...I've accepted.'

There was a long, deafening silence, then Fee said in an appalled voice, 'But you can't, Maddy, not over the phone. You don't know him, or anything about him, you don't know what you're letting yourself in for, you've got to have a job description, it's mandatory...' She trailed off.

'He's given me a verbal job description and is sending a printed copy through the post. It sounds just what I want—busy, steady, but not too pressurised. There are three partners. It's near the moors, and that's just what I need right now—space, room to breathe.'

She looked at the closed expressions on their concerned faces and felt almost criminal for deserting them. 'Try to understand,' she pleaded. 'It's on a three-month trial basis and if we don't suit each other I'll be back soon after the baby's arrived, Fee.'

'And if you do suit?'

'I'll be up for the christening, or earlier if you want me—promise.' She produced a tentative smile. 'Come on, you two, give me your blessing or whatever,' she said wryly.

There was another little silence, then Fee grinned. 'Oh, come on, then, you daft creature, let's give you a kiss and a hug.' Heaving herself to her feet, she trundled round the table and did just that.

Laughing, Madeleine came up for air. 'Wow,' she said. 'It's a bit like being smothered by a fat pillow.'

'Do you mind?' said Fee haughtily. 'Not fat—nicely rounded with child.'

'If you say so,' giggled Madeleine.

Naomi topped up Fee's glass with mineral water, and her own and Madeleine's with wine. She touched Maddy's glass with her own. 'Here's looking at you, kid,' she said, in her best Humphrey Bogart style—she was a devotee of old forties films—and added, 'Go and slay 'em in the wilds of Cornwall.'

And I'm going to do just that, thought Madeleine later, lying in bed and reflecting on the evening's events. There had been the totally unexpected phone call from Dr Trellawney and her impulsive acceptance of his offer of the job. And Fee's and Naomi's equally unexpected reaction. She'd expected surprise, but hadn't expected that they'd be so shattered and see her move to 'the sticks', as they had put it, as almost a betrayal of their friendship.

It was concern, of course, that had made them react as they had, but all had been well in the end after she'd been able to reassure them on several points, gleaned from her conversation with the doctor. The accommodation offered was not a dingy bedsitter, as they'd scathingly assumed, but a self-contained, furnished flat over the main surgery in the village of St Kellier's. It was hers for a peppercorn rent, with free electricity and water thrown in, more than making up for the small drop in the salary that they'd agreed.

'And why is it important that you have your own transport?' Naomi had wanted to know. 'Are you expected to ferry patients around or something?'

'No, though I sometimes might have to make some home visits but I shall get an allowance for that. Chiefly,

it's because the nearest large town is Penruth, twelve
miles away, and there's an infrequent bus service.'

Naomi and Fee had groaned dramatically and rolled
their eyes heavenwards. 'It's the end of the world,'
they'd said, shaking their heads in despair. 'Oh, Maddy,
how could you? You must be out of your tiny mind.'

There were times over the next few weeks, as she
worked out her notice, arranged to let her flat and finally
said her goodbyes to Kits, when Maddy wondered if
they could be right. Apart from the fact that all her colleagues agreed with Fee and Naomi that she was com-
mitting herself to near oblivion, she was touched by the
genuine regret that everyone expressed at her departure.

Somehow over recent months she hadn't thought anyone cared any more, that the old team spirit had died.
But now she wasn't sure. Not that it mattered. The die
was cast, and she was Cornwall-bound in the new year.

CHAPTER TWO

MADELEINE brought Genevieve Two to a halt on the summit of a low, rounded hill and peered out through the curtain of softly drifting snow.

She consulted her map and patted the polished wooden dashboard. 'Well done, Gen, we've made it. We've arrived. This is St Kellier's.'

Although she had been on the road since six that morning, she didn't feel particularly tired but rather elated. Her stomach churned with excited, if slightly apprehensive anticipation as she looked down on the village sprawled out below. This was to be her home and place of work for the immediate future.

Always provided, she reminded herself wryly, that she and her new colleagues, and especially Dr Trellawney—she had a gut feeling that he would be the one to please—were mutually acceptable to each other. It was a step into the unknown, exchanging a large city hospital for a country practice and a handful of strangers headed by the doctor.

What, she wondered, not for the first time since she'd been accepted for the job, would he be like, not only physically but, more importantly, to work with? Would he be easygoing and friendly, hard to please or arrogant and bossy?

His letters hadn't provided a clue. They had been polite and to the point, as had his single phone call when he had offered her the job, though his voice, slightly drawling and soft, had belied the terseness of his words. Or was she kidding herself? She was a sucker for deep, melodious voices.

Well, the answers were down there in the village. It was no good to put off the moment of truth—the sooner she got moving the better. She put Genevieve into low gear and cautiously, slithering a little on the freezing film of snow, made her way down the narrow, winding lane to St Kellier's.

It was larger than she had imagined. House- and streetlights were on, glimmering through the early dusk, though it was only three-thirty. They were cheerful and inviting after the bleakness of the moors she had just crossed. A ribbon of amber lights and well-lit small shops identified the main road—Pilgrim Street—where, Dr Trellawney had informed her in a businesslike letter, 'you will find The Old House and the medical centre some five hundred yards down on the left-hand side as you enter from the top end of the village'.

The letter continued:

> Drive straight into the staff car park, which separates The Old House, my private residence, from the centre. Call at the house and, if I'm not available, my housekeeper, Mrs Gumbrill, will make you welcome until my return. I look forward to meeting you. Yours sincerely, Stewart Trellawney.

'Why a housekeeper and not a wife?' she'd wondered aloud to Fee and Naomi.

'Perhaps he's a crusty old bachelor who likes to be waited on hand and foot by a trusted ancient retainer who guards him with her life,' Fee had suggested.

'Or a randy old widower, who employs a glamorous young housekeeper to provide *all* his creature comforts,' Naomi had surmised with a sly grin.

There was nothing glamorous about the lady, whom she presumed to be Mrs Gumbrill, who opened the door of The Old House to her on that bitterly cold January afternoon. Naomi was obviously wrong about the randy old widower. Dumpy, unsmiling, with wispy grey hair scraped up into a knot, she surveyed Madeleine through small, expressionless black eyes set like sloes in her pasty face.

She stood four-square and silent in the doorway as if on guard—Fee's faithful old retainer to the letter. If the rest of Fee's prediction was true, Dr Trellawney would be a spoilt old man with a chip on his shoulder.

Surely not, with that voice. And his letter had been courteous, although wrong about the welcome from his housekeeper—there was nothing remotely welcoming about her.

That's all I need—a housekeeper like something out of a du Maurier novel, thought Madeleine. She pinned a smile on her face. 'Mrs Gumbrill?' she asked politely.

The woman nodded. 'And you'll be the new nurse, Miss Coleman?'

'I am, indeed,' replied Madeleine cheerfully.

'Then you'd better come in,' said the woman. Thin, buttoned-up lips twitched into a semblance of a smile. 'I dare say you could do with a cup of tea.'

'Thank you, I could murder one,' said Madeleine, as she stepped into the large, square, white-panelled hall. 'Oh, this is lovely,' she exclaimed, surprised by its simple perfection. 'So warm. And the flowers—the scent is gorgeous.' Impulsively she bent over the large, colourful bowl of mixed spring bulbs, standing on a polished side table, and inhaled deeply.

'The scent is mostly from the hyacinths,' said a man's voice from behind her.

Her spine tingled. There was no mistaking the voice—it belonged to Dr Trellawney. He must have come in hot on her heels, quickly and quietly, giving no warning.

On a little gasp of surprise Madeleine murmured rather breathlessly, as she straightened, 'Oh.' She turned to face him, preparing herself for... She wasn't quite sure what—not Naomi's randy old man, but Fee's crusty old bachelor perhaps?

He stood just inside the doorway, a large, bulky man, who towered over the dumpy Mrs Gumbrill. *She* had a startled expression on her face, and had clearly also been taken unawares by his sudden appearance.

Madeleine found herself looking up into piercing, smoky-grey eyes in a lean, powerful face. Her first thought was that he might be crusty but he certainly wasn't old. There wasn't a fleck of white in his thick black hair, except where a flake or two of snow had settled. Her second thought was that he had a lovely mouth, wide and tender, matching the honey-gold voice not the cool eyes...

She snapped to attention. Dear God, what was she thinking?

She felt the blood surge up into her cheeks and half turned and bent again over the flower-bowl, waiting for the embarrassing blush to subside. 'It's gorgeous,' she repeated inanely. 'The scent.'

'As you say, gorgeous.' A faint, sardonic smile curled at the corners of the wide mouth. He stretched out his hand. Madeleine put hers into it. It was long-fingered, warm, firm, reassuring. They shook hands. His eyes remained chilly but the smile widened slightly. 'Stewart Trellawney,' he said formally.

'Madeleine Coleman.' She was equally formal.

The front door was closed with a loud, decisive snap.

He turned a bland face to his housekeeper. 'Tea, please, Mrs Gumbrill, sandwiches, scones and some of your luscious fruit cake.'

'Very well, Doctor.' Her voice was grudging, and with a curt nod she turned and disappeared down a wide passage, leading from the hall to the rear of the house.

It seemed to Madeleine that there was disapproval in every line of her dumpy little body.

'I don't think your housekeeper approves of me,' she said, trying to sound casual and cheerful but feeling suddenly saddened by the woman's unpleasant attitude and the doctor's formality.

Was this the way all strangers were treated in St Kellier's? Had she made a ghastly mistake, coming here? An unexpected wave of longing for her friends and Kits, with all its faults, washed over her. She hoped it didn't show in her face.

The doctor frowned. 'Mrs Gumbrill doesn't approve of anybody much. Please don't let it worry you.'

Madeleine felt a twinge of alarm. Had he noticed her moment of weakness? Did he think that she was frightened of his old besom of a housekeeper? It would make her appear pretty wimpish— not a good impression to make on a new employer. She must squash that idea, pronto.

She said quickly and confidently, 'Oh, I'm not worried. Mrs Gumbrill may be a bit formidable but nothing compared to some of the belligerent bag ladies I've had to deal with. Now, they really are tough old birds.'

That should satisfy him. She challenged him with her dark amber eyes, conscious that they were her best feature. Tiger eyes, an admirer had once labelled them. 'You know,' he'd said, 'as in the poem, ''Tiger, tiger, burning bright''—fierce and intelligent.'

Would the doctor see them like that? she wondered.

His mouth quirked into a sudden, lopsided smile. He raised one eyebrow and a hint of a smile actually touched his smoky-grey eyes. 'Indeed, a formidable old lady but, as you say, one you can easily cope with with all your experience. Not that you'll be seeing much of her. She helps clean the surgery block occasionally, but otherwise your paths are unlikely to cross.'

'Sounds like an ideal working relationship,' said Madeleine lightly.

'As you say—ideal.' His voice was dry, but he was still smiling. 'Now, let's make ourselves comfortable in the parlour while we're waiting for tea.'

It was a beautiful smile, thought Madeleine, nothing like the chilly, formal smile with which he'd greeted her. This one warmed his arctic eyes and lit up his whole face—a smile of approval.

Great! If he'd noticed her moment of weakness he was reassured. But she mustn't relax. She must be on her mettle—he wouldn't miss a thing.

Madeleine returned his smile. 'Tea sounds marvellous but, if I might use your cloakroom first, I've been travelling since six and feel a bit of a mess.'

His eyes swept over her in a shrewd, assessing glance, coming to rest on her boyishly cut, smooth, thick cap of tawny fair hair. Amusement flared in them for an instant. 'You don't look it.' His voice, too, was amused. 'There's not a strand out of place.'

He lifted his hand, and for one wild, pulse-quickening moment she thought he was going to smooth her hair...

Of course he did no such thing, but gestured across the hall. 'The cloakroom's over there,' he said, his other hand on the brass knob of the door beside him. 'Do take your time. I'll be waiting for you in here when you're ready.'

She did take her time—less to touch up her make-up and run a comb through her cropped hair than to make some sense of her unexpected response to the enigmatic doctor. He'd rattled her from the moment he'd walked into the hall behind her. She'd expected an elderly, perhaps crotchety, country doctor, not a cool, self-possessed man, at a guess in his late thirties.

Peering into the mirror above the basin, she pressed her palms against her flushed cheeks. Why had she ex-

pected him to touch her hair and—even more disconcerting *why*, when he hadn't, had she felt a quiver of
disappointment? It was a ridiculous reaction to a man
she had only just met.

And why on earth had she made such an effort to
convince him that she wasn't upset by his unpleasant
housekeeper, but was a highly efficient, capable nurse,
used to holding her own? Her references told him that,
and he would find it out for himself when she started
work. Why had she wanted to justify herself to him?

She gave a snort of self-derision. For heaven's sake,
stop all this soul-searching, she told herself sharply. Put
it down to nerves. Not surprising, really, never having
worked anywhere but Kits. Get a grip on yourself,
woman.

She took a long steadying breath, squared her shoulders and let herself out of the cloakroom, all geared up
for her second confrontation with her new boss.

For a second or two, unobserved, she stood silently in
the open doorway of the sitting room. Dr Trellawney
was standing with his hands in his trouser pockets and
his long legs apart with his back to the fireplace, looking
remote and deep in thought, his mouth set in a straight
line.

Without his bulky car coat, he looked very tall and
lean in a blue ribbed sweater worn over a striped blue
shirt and tie. Although he was lean, he was not thin. His
shoulders and thighs looked sinewy and muscular, a
match for any of the rugger men at Kits. He was good
to look at, but what of the man beneath the skin?

Suddenly aware of Madeleine's presence, he snapped
out of his reverie and with a few long strides crossed
the room. 'Do come and sit down,' he said, taking her
elbow and steering her to a deep armchair by the crackling log fire.

Madeleine ignored the slight tingle where his fingers rested.

'Thank you,' she murmured, as she sank into the well-upholstered seat.

He folded himself into the armchair at the other side of the fireplace.

'The tea's just arrived,' he said. 'We'll give it a few minutes to draw.'

The low table between them was laden with fine china and white linen napkins. A large fruit cake on a silver stand was flanked by a covered dish—crumpets, she guessed. There were also plates of scones and sandwiches, and dishes of cream, jam and pâté.

It was all very gracious, a bit unnerving in its perfection, she thought, glancing quickly about her. Obviously Mrs Gumbrill, however unpleasant, did the doctor proud when it came to food and the care of his household. Everything gleamed in the lamp- and firelight.

It was a rich room, the kind seen on a Dickensian Christmas card, with the blazing fire in the wide fireplace, dark red velvet curtains at the windows, plump red cushions on the various brocade-covered easy chairs and sofas dotted about the large room.

Like the hall, it was beautifully proportioned and panelled in white—a striking contrast to the heavy furnishings and occasional tables, crowded with potted plants and numerous ornaments. A curious mixture of clean-cut Georgian lines and Victorian opulence.

Madeleine was surprised. The room, at least the Victorian part of it, didn't match the doctor. Why was a rather austere man like him surrounded by fiddly bric-à-brac? The two just didn't go together.

He noticed her surprise and must have guessed at the reason.

'A legacy from my predecessor, Dr Marric...' he waved a hand to indicate the crowded tables '...and his before him—family heirlooms. There've been Marric doctors here for generations.'

'Oh... But you're not a Marric.' Why on earth had she said that so baldly? It sounded almost like an accusation. She wished she could take it back.

'No.' A curious expression flitted across the sculpted lines of his face, his grey eyes, reflecting the blue of his shirt, softened and appeared for a moment to be tinged with sadness. 'No, I'm not a Marric, but I do my best to keep up the family tradition.'

Was she imagining it, or was there a slight bitterness in his voice? She was puzzled. Why did his eyes look sad—because he wasn't a Marric? Ridiculous! A name couldn't mean that much. But he had spoken of family tradition so he had to have some connection with them.

'Are you...related?' she asked tentatively.

'No.' He was curt. 'Just a one-time colleague, *trying* to carry on where my predecessor left off.'

The hint of bitterness was there again. Or was it pain—or was she imagining it? Why '*trying*', as if he was afraid of failing? And hard on that thought came another. Perhaps one day he'll confide in me... She went hot and cold. How could she entertain such an idea, sitting opposite this man who was practically a stranger? But a peculiar little glow of pleasure trickled through her at the possibility.

She squashed it. She was shaken to the core by her reaction to this puzzling man, who had something on his mind that was clearly tied up with his work. Not, she guessed, the usual problems that beset any GP. It was more complicated than that, but what? Inwardly she gave a grim little smile.

It was ironic that she'd left Kits partly to escape from the frustrations of working in an atmosphere where rumour was rife and competition fierce, only to find that this rural backwater had undercurrents of its own—an old harridan of a housekeeper and a polite, reserved boss, who played his cards close to his chest and clearly resented any intrusion into his private life. He was probably already regretting the little he had revealed.

So why did she want to reach out and comfort him— find out what that fleeting, haunted look was all about? She banished the thought as it was born. You didn't go around offering reassurance to a self-contained man like the doctor, she reminded herself.

Madeleine felt she had to say something to break the small silence that had settled between them. She said abruptly, 'I'm looking forward to working for you and your partners, Dr Trellawney. It's going to be a challenging experience.'

His eyes met hers, unreadable, no longer sad.

'You're dead right, it will be.' His voice was flat. 'We're a busy practice, serving a wide area, and increasingly we're offering more on-the-spot treatment. That's why we wanted a nurse with your sort of experience, used to up-to-date equipment and methods. Our current nurse, Phyllis Taylor, can't really cope with the extra work.'

'Does she mind you engaging another nurse? I'd hate her to feel that I was muscling in on her territory.'

He chuckled. 'Phyllis? No way, she's not that kind of person. She doesn't mind in the least. In fact, she's looking forward to having help. Nice woman, jolly good nurse, bit stuck in her ways, but none the worse for that. Hates computer work, due to retire soon. She'll be much missed.'

It was a surprisingly warm reference from the reserved doctor. A good omen, perhaps! 'I look forward to meeting her.'

He was brisk. 'You will tomorrow. Now, let's have tea, and then I'll take you over to the flat and leave you to sort yourself out.' He leaned over the table and picked up the elegant Queen Anne teapot. 'I'm sure you're ready for this.' He filled a cup and handed it to her. 'Do help yourself to milk or lemon, and whatever—and you must be hungry. Try the crumpets. They're made by the local bakery, and are scrumptious with Mrs Gumbrill's home-made pâté.'

He didn't attempt to make small talk as they ate, although he was the perfect host, making sure that her plate and cup were constantly filled. Madeleine wasn't sorry. She'd only snacked at the stops she'd made on the journey, and was only too ready to fill up on the delicious food set before her.

And so, apparently, was the doctor, who was eating with obvious relish, his strong, steady fingers efficiently quartering and buttering crumpets with neat precision. Bet he's good with a scalpel, she thought. Wonder how often he gets a chance to use one?

Her job description had mentioned that the practice carried out minor surgical procedures, but how minor and how frequently? she wondered. Did they hold elective surgery sessions or just treat anyone who wandered in, rather like a casualty department?

She was still speculating on this and was about to ask when Dr. Trellawney leaned back in his chair, gave a sigh of satisfaction and said almost apologetically, 'Lord, that's better. I needed food. I was absolutely ravenous and my blood sugar was near zero. I missed lunch—had an emergency call-out.'

He was looking calm and relaxed. No wonder he'd been spiky, he'd been hungry. This was more like it—work talk. They'd be on the same wavelength.

'What sort of an emergency?' Madeleine asked, and leaned forward, wanting to know the details.

He didn't seem surprised by her eagerness—looked rather pleased, in fact.

'Farm worker in a tractor that turned over, pinning

him down. Partly severed his thigh and fractured his femur. Comminuted fracture—nasty mess. Did what I could to control the bleeding, immobilise the limb and treat for shock, whilst waiting for the ambulance to arrive. There was some delay so I stayed with the poor chap to run some fluids into him and keep him warm, which was a bit of a problem in this weather in an open field.

'In other words, applied the basic drill for shock and haemorrhage—well, you know all about that.'

Madeleine pulled a face. 'Certainly do, though I've never had to do it in a field in a snowstorm and I've never dealt with a tractor injury—you don't get many of those in central London.' She tilted a smile at him. 'But I've dealt with plenty of smashed-up legs after the paramedics have been in action. They're brilliant at keeping casualties going till they can get them to us, and that's what you're talking about, isn't it—high-powered first aiding till an accident victim can be hospitalised?'

Dr Trellawney nodded. 'Yep. Our patients often call us first, knowing that an ambulance has to come from miles away and might not be immediately available or could be delayed in bad weather, crossing the moors. That's why we're each kitted out with an emergency bag with a drip set, glucose and saline, polarised blanket, pressure bandages, inflatable splints, mobile oxygen mask and various painkillers and stimulants.'

He grinned and arched a brow. 'Real front-line lifesaving stuff,' he said in a dry voice, seeing her expression. 'Surprised, Miss Coleman, that an out-of-the-way place like St Kellier's in the depths of rural Cornwall is technically on the ball?'

Was he gently teasing or being sarcastic, mocking her ignorance of country ways—accusing her of being a sophisticated townee? Her eyes locked with his as she tried to read their blue-grey depths. For a moment they stared steadily at each other in silence over the gleaming silver on the table.

A log shifted in the fireplace.

Damn the man—was he deliberately trying to rile her? If only she knew what he was thinking—he gave so little away. He *had* surprised her, and seemed to be enjoying it.

She took a deep breath, and said in a taut, over-polite voice, 'Yes, Doctor, I *am* surprised, not because I think that medicine here is somehow inferior but because you have to be a skilled paramedic as well as a GP. I've always thought of GPs as sitting in their surgeries, diagnosing, prescribing and making house calls, not haring round the countryside equipped for major emergencies.'

'And you'd be right where many practices are concerned—the bulk of the work *is* in surgery, but because of our geographic location we have to be prepared for anything. We're not isolated so much by distance as by the terrain and the weather. Seldom snow...' he waved a hand toward the curtained window '...but fog, rolling off the moors, steep, winding lanes, shortage of ambulances.

'Our priority is getting to a patient in time and being prepared for anything—can be a matter of life and death. Sounds dramatic, but it's true.'

He wasn't being sarcastic or teasing now, but deadly serious. In a low, diffident voice she said, 'I've a lot to learn about a country practice, haven't I? I'd no idea. I feel totally inadequate.'

Again taking her by surprise and making her pulse skip a beat, he stretched across the table and touched her hand, lightly, briefly, and in an unexpectedly gentle voice murmured, 'So did I when I came here. It takes some getting used to, a practice like this. You just have to work at it—hang in there—but, as with all medicine, it has its own rewards.'

His wrist-watch beeped. He looked down at it, then up again to meet her eyes. He smiled his wide, generous smile, which transformed his stern features and made her catch her breath. 'Surgery in ten minutes. If you're ready, I'll take your things up to the flat and see you safely installed.'

She stood at once. 'No, please don't do that. I can manage if you point me in the right direction.'

He rose too. 'No way,' he said. 'There's an inch or two of snow out there, and a slippery outside staircase to negotiate to the flat, which is above the surgery block. I'd hate to find you laid out at the foot of it.'

It took nearly a quarter of an hour to transfer her numerous bags, boxes and suitcases from Genevieve to the flat. He's right, Madeleine thought as she hurried up the steps with her final load—a carrier bag full of goodies that Fee had provided from their favourite Italian delicatessen and a brilliant red poinsettia, a farewell gift from Naomi—it is slippery.

Light spilled from the doorway above her, illuminating the circular staircase that led up into the flat from the courtyard below. She skidded on the impacted snow as she reached the little platform at the top of the stairs. A hand shot out and grabbed her.

'You shouldn't have rushed,' said the doctor, pulling her none too gently over the doorstep into the kitchen.

She panted. 'You're already late for surgery.'

He shrugged. 'For once nobody will mind. They'll know that I've been welcoming the new nurse and be all agog for the latest info on both you and Joe Black, the tractor casualty.'

'How on earth do they know about him or me?'

'By a kind of osmosis. Village gossip beats the hospital grapevine any day.'

'Oh, I see.' But she didn't really. It had been a long time since she'd lived on the Kent farm where she'd spent some of her childhood, and she'd forgotten about the gossip.

His eyes glinted. 'Don't look so shattered, Miss Coleman. You'll get used to living in a fish-bowl—I have.' He took the carrier bag and the poinsettia from her and dumped them on the working surface beside the fridge. 'Now, let me show you around the flat before I go—it won't take a minute. It is, you might say, compact rather than spacious, but I think you'll find it comfortable enough.

'By the way, Karen stocked up the fridge and some of the cupboards with the basics, though I see you've come provided.'

'But not with basics, if I know my friend, Fee.' Madeleine laughed. 'Probably wild strawberries and something exotic in aspic.'

The doctor raised an ironic eyebrow. 'Oh, a generous but frivolous friend, with plenty of cash to splash around?'

'You couldn't be more wrong. She's a super-efficient, hard-working theatre sister, currently pregnant, happily married to an orthopaedic registrar, not very rich and definitely not frivolous—just generous.'

'Hell! I walked into that one, didn't I? Sorry.'

'Not to worry. By the way, who's Karen?'

'Our practice manager.'

'Manager! Really! Can't imagine any manager I've ever met, filling a fridge for a lowly employee.'

'Karen's not any manager. She was secretary and senior bookkeeper-receptionist here for years, but took a manager's course to satisfy the authorities. She's highly efficient, but hasn't lost the common touch and tends to mother us all. Now—' he was suddenly brisk '—for your tour of inspection.'

Dr Trellawney led the way from the neat modern kitchen, with its range of wall cupboards, into a long, low sitting room, furnished, Madeleine guessed, with cast-offs from The Old House.

There was a polished round table and three elegant, elderly dining chairs, two rather shabby but comfortable-looking armchairs, an electric fire with artificial coals and a combined glass-fronted bookcase and bureau, *circa* 1930s. There were rugs on the polished wood floor and a large window overlooked the courtyard, draped with fading, heavy, brocade curtains.

It had definite possibilities, she thought as she gazed around her, in her mind's eye replacing the heavy curtains with bright, chintzy ones and recovering the armchairs. She would enjoy doing that, just as she had enjoyed furnishing her London home... Her stomach churned—bad idea, thinking of that.

She became aware that the doctor was speaking.

'And from here,' he said, piloting her toward the window, 'you can watch all the comings and goings—keep track of who's on or off duty.'

They stood side by side, gazing down on the lamp-lit car park. They were close, almost touching—he smelt of woody-scented soap or aftershave, and fresh air. Willing herself not to tremble and him not to notice, Maddy inched away from his side.

'A bird's-eye view,' she said brightly.

'Exactly.' He closed the heavy curtains, turned smartly and crossed the room to open a door that led into a narrow corridor.

'Bedroom and bathroom,' he explained, pointing to the two doors opposite. 'And this...' he strode down the corridor '...opens onto the stairs down to the surgery block—your back entrance, you might say.'

He stopped, produced a key from his trouser pocket and unlocked the door, then handed the key to her. 'This,' he said, 'you guard with your life. Lock the door after you whenever you go out. Security precautions, should anyone break into the flat and try to gain entry to the surgery.'

'Thanks,' she replied tartly as she took it from him. 'Do you think that's very likely?'

'It hasn't happened yet.' He looked down at her, his cool eyes searching her face. 'You're not nervous, are you?' he asked.

'Not a bit.'

'Good, but if you're bothered any time you can always get me on the internal or external phone—the numbers are on the wall in the kitchen.'

'I hope I'll never have to use them.'

He nodded. 'Of course.' He opened the door to the surgery stairs, and a faint hum of muffled distant voices, coughs and ringing telephones filtered upwards.

Madeleine found it surprisingly reassuring—it was nice to know there were other people around. 'Sounds like you have plenty of customers,' she said.

'So what's new?' He stepped out onto the small landing at the top of the spiral staircase. 'Lock up after me,' he said. 'I'll see you at eight tomorrow, show you around and introduce you to everyone. You don't have to work—take time to get acclimatised. My room's the third on the right from the foot of the stairs opposite Reception.'

'I'll be there *and* ready to start work.'

'As you will.' He nodded again and started down the stairs, but paused at the third step. 'And welcome to St Kellier's, Miss Coleman. I hope you'll enjoy working here.'

The words were all right and he sounded sincere, but if only he would unbend, smile again before he left, relax as he had after tea. She murmured, 'Thank you, and...'

'Yes?' He hovered on the stairs. His thick black hair gleamed, the stern lines of his face were thrown into relief by the light from above and his eyes were deep wells beside his prominent, aristocratic nose.

'The name's Madeleine.'

There was a moment's silence, then his mouth twitched at the corners into a near smile. 'I know,' he drawled softly. 'Goodnight, Madeleine, sleep well.'

He raised his hand in salute, turned unhurriedly, descended the rest of the stairs and disappeared from her line of sight.

'And goodnight to you, too, Dr Stewart Trellawney,' she muttered as she closed and locked the door. 'Just you wait. One day I'll find out what's bugging you.'

CHAPTER THREE

MADELEINE wound her way down the spiral staircase at seven-forty the following morning. She was too early for her appointment with Dr Trellawney but she couldn't stay in the flat a moment longer. Her stomach was full of butterflies and adrenaline pumped through her body at a great rate. She wanted to get on with the day, get cracking on her new job.

'Good morning, Sister.'

The doctor's voice floated up from the foot of the staircase. Her breath caught in her throat. 'Oh.' She paused and peered down between the twisty, black iron bannisters, took a ragged breath and said huskily, 'Good morning.'

'Sorry, did I startle you?'

He had, but she said, 'No.' She circled down a little further.

'Did you sleep well?'

Was it a meaningless politeness, or did he really want to know? He sounded detached and formal, as he had yesterday. She had hoped that they might start off the morning on a warmer note after his wry but amicable departure last night.

She reached the bottom step and paused there, her face on a level with his. His grey eyes surveyed her appraisingly, and she was glad that she had taken care with her make-up to conceal the smudges beneath her own eyes.

With cool composure she returned his appraising look. He needed a shave—his square jaw was dark with stubble and he was wearing the bulky car coat that he'd worn yesterday evening. It didn't take a Chief Inspector Morse to deduce that he'd been out and about in the small hours.

'I slept like a log,' she lied cheerfully. No way would she admit to lying awake, wondering what on earth she was doing in rural Cornwall about to start working for a reserved enigma of a man who held some sort of peculiar attraction for her. 'But you—you haven't slept much. Presumably you were called out.'

He rubbed his fingers over his bristly chin and pulled a face. 'Is it that obvious?' He shrugged. 'That's babies for you. They choose to arrive at the most ungodly hours, especially if they decide to beat the clock.'

'So you had an emergency on your hands? Quite scary, I would have thought, delivering a baby at home with no back-up or anything.'

His high forehead creased as he lifted his brows into surprised arches. 'No, not scary, but on alert. But this was a planned home delivery, not an emergency. The infant just decided to jump the gun by a week. The midwife and I worked together—no problems, everything went as expected. Nice little baby—a boy, Joseph. Everything in working order, all the right number of fingers and toes and reflexes. Sensible parents who followed all the rules to prepare for his arrival. He'll do very well.'

She still couldn't quite believe that it had been as straightforward as he'd suggested. 'You must be relieved, though, especially as he was early.'

He grinned. 'It was a good result.'

She scrabbled in her memory for what she'd learned when she'd done her stint on Maternity when she was training.

'But don't premature babies have to go into incubators?'

'Only if they are very premature, much underweight or have breathing or other obvious problems. Master

Joseph, I'm happy to say, appears to be as fit as a fiddle, a perfect little specimen. He was feeding happily when I left, all set to rule that particular roost for a long time to come.'

He was so sure of himself—pleased, almost smug.

'Do you do many home deliveries?' she asked curiously. Everyone she knew went into high-tech maternity units to have their babies, with a skilled team to hand—obstetricians, paediatricians and such. She'd heard of women giving birth in all sorts of unlikely places—indeed, they'd had a couple in A and E—but only by accident, never by design.

'A fair number, and rising. Home births are catching on. Why—surprised?'

'Yes. What happens if something goes wrong?'

'Hasn't happened yet with any of our planned deliveries. We have regular clinics, keep a close check before and after birth, do scans, brief the parents. Any problem and they'd be whipped into the Royal in Penruth, but to date that hasn't happened. All our home births have been happy occasions. One day you must see for yourself.'

'But—'

The opening of a door at one end of the long corridor and a flurry of voices interrupted their conversation. Two women came through the doorway and stood just inside, stamping snow off their booted feet.

The doctor called, 'Good morning, ladies.'

'Morning, Doctor,' they called back.

They began walking slowly along the corridor, and Madeleine was aware that she was being sized up as they drew nearer. She stepped down to the floor and stumbled. Dr Trellawney took her arm. She felt herself stiffen, then consciously made herself relax.

Immediately he released her—because he'd noticed? He said in a quiet voice, 'We'll finish our conversation some other time. Right now, let's go and meet Phyllis and Karen.'

He made the introductions briskly as they stood outside the staffroom. 'This is Phyllis Taylor, your nursing partner, and Karen Foster, our manager—and this, ladies, as you must have guessed, is Madeleine Coleman, your new colleague.'

They shook hands and mouthed polite words at each other.

The doctor inclined his head toward Madeleine, met her eyes and smiled into them. 'Good luck,' he said. 'Hope you enjoy your day. Phyllis and Karen will take care of you. I'll be off. I want to snatch a shower and shave before surgery.' Turning, he walked with long, easy strides away down the corridor.

It was absurd, but Madeleine wanted to cry out, Don't go. Feeling foolish and curiously bereft, she allowed herself to be ushered into the staffroom by her two colleagues.

'The good doctor, brief and to the point as usual,' said Phyllis, giving Madeleine a friendly grin as she divested herself of her outdoor clothes. She replaced her headscarf with a starched uniform cap and anchored it firmly into place. 'I know caps went out with the ark,' she said, seeing Madeleine's startled expression, 'but I'm of the old school and don't feel dressed without one.'

She was tall and thin, with a long, humorous face. Everything about her was neat, from her carefully arranged greying hair, topped with the lacy cap, to her navy blue belted uniform dress and well polished duty shoes, which she had exchanged for her boots. It was clear from this opening remark that the doctor had been right. Phyllis Taylor was an old-fashioned sort of nurse, dedicated and caring but wary of some of the technical developments in medicine.

Immediately confirming this, she said with another

grin, 'It's great to have you aboard. I'm too long in the tooth to take on some of this newfangled equipment. I'm strictly the hands-on type. Give me a bandage or a syringe and I know where I am, but you can keep your computers and suchlike—they're all yours. You take care of all that, and we'll get along like a house on fire.'

Her down-to-earth attitude was comforting and cheering, and Madeleine found herself grinning back at her. 'Fair enough,' she said, 'as long as I can do my share of hands-on stuff. I like it, too.'

By contrast to Phyllis, Karen Foster was short, plump, bouncy and pretty, with a wealth of curly brown hair. Obviously no slave to fashion, she was wearing a brilliant multicoloured cardigan over a clashing jazzy sweater, which moulded itself to her ample bosom.

Although, at a guess, only in her thirties, she was rather like a bossy little robin redbreast or a mother hen, chivvying her chicks—just as Dr Trellawney had described.

Madeleine thanked her for stocking up the fridge in the flat.

'Think nothing of it,' she said cheerfully. 'All part of the service. It was the least I could do. We didn't know what time you'd get here and the stores close at six, except on a Friday when they're open till eight.'

'Well, it was nice of you to bother. I must settle up. What do I owe you?'

'Nothing. The boss said it was on the house, a sort of welcome to St Kellier's.'

'That was kind of him.'

'He's a kind man,' said Karen.

'The best,' added Phyllis laconically, to Madeleine's surprise.

The rest of the morning had a breathless quality about it as Madeleine was given a whirlwind tour of the centre.

Used to the vastness of Kits, she mastered the layout of the building without difficulty. It was built in an E-shape round the courtyard car park, facing The Old House. The reception area was in the middle, consulting and treatment rooms in the two longer arms.

Pinning names to faces was another matter. The centre, which served many surrounding villages, was bustling. The receptionists were too busy to do more than nod as they answered the phone and ushered patients in and out. And the names and faces of the district nurses who appeared remained a blur. Apparently, they were employed by the county, but they had an office in the building and co-ordinated with the centre staff.

Over a late coffee in the staffroom Phyllis introduced her to the physiotherapist, Betty Boxer, who was holding a clinic that day. There were other auxiliary practitioners who worked part time—a massage therapist, counsellor, chiropodist and optician.

'Patients are treated here,' explained Phyllis, 'because many of them have difficulty getting into Penruth. They haven't all got cars and the bus service is abysmal.'

It was a far cry from the quiet country practice of her imaginings, Madeleine thought, trying to absorb all the new names and snippets of information she was receiving. Surely there couldn't be many more people for her to meet.

She said as much to Phyllis when the room emptied and they found themselves alone, finishing their coffee.

'Well, there are the two other partners,' observed Phyllis in her dry manner. 'Together with Dr Trellawney, they are by way of being our employers.'

'Good lord, how awful—I'd almost forgotten them. Dr Trellawney seems to be—'

'Very much the boss, bit autocratic, confidence personified.'

Madeleine nodded. Tall, lean, a little remote, he came over as exactly that. 'Exactly,' she said. 'The boss man.'

'Well, he is since old Dr Marric died. He stepped into his shoes and automatically the role of head of practice, although Mike Roach and Alison Peachey are, in fact, equal partners. But he's had loads more experience in a busy city practice.' She frowned. 'Look, you may find him a bit aloof at times but take no notice—he's a super doctor and one hundred per cent dependable.'

Madeleine thought of the battle for top jobs at St Kits, medical and nursing, and asked, 'But didn't his partners mind him taking over?'

'No. Neither of them wanted the responsibility, and he's a natural—a workaholic. Besides, it's what the old doctor wanted.' She laughed. 'And he was the law around here. I should know, I worked for him for years.' She stood and looked at her fob-watch. 'We'd better get cracking. I'll make sure you meet Alison and Mike before the day is out.'

In fact, they met them only moments later as they were leaving the staffroom and the doctors were entering. They both seemed pleasant enough as they shook hands and welcomed Maddy to St Kellier's, but there was time only to exchange names as they were all in a hurry—Phyllis and Madeleine to get on with their heavy list and the doctors to snatch quick coffees, before going off on their rounds.

Madeleine liked Alison Peachey immediately, but wasn't too sure about Mike Roach. His handshake was almost too firm and lingering. Alison was probably in her early thirties, but looked younger, a pretty woman with long blonde hair caught at her nape.

'Just married and not long back from her honeymoon,' Phyllis informed her when they were back in the treatment room, 'and happily playing house. But a good, dedicated doctor when she comes down off cloud nine. You'll get on fine with our Alison.'

'And Dr Roach?' Madeleine asked. She guessed he was about forty—he had sandy fair hair, a boyishly handsome face and oodles of charm.

'Mike!' Phyllis wrinkled her long, narrow nose. 'He's OK, not a bad doctor, bit of a playboy. He's got a super wife and two nice kids. Charms the ladies, not always so hot with the men, though he never neglects anyone— but there are times when it's obvious that he'd rather be out surfing or skin-diving than in his consulting room.'

'But generally reliable?'

'Generally,' said Phyllis drily. 'Just don't fall for his charms or let him get away with anything.' She looked vaguely uncomfortable. 'Basically sound but I think he sometimes forgets he's married so just watch it.'

'I will,' promised Maddy, equally drily—she'd met his type before. She was grateful to Phyllis for giving the warning, liking her the more for having given it reluctantly and not maliciously.

As well as the staff, there were patients for her to meet—dozens, from the moment Phyllis opened up for business at nine. Some were already booked in, but as the morning wore on others were referred by the doctors for dressings, blood or urine tests or injections and had to be sandwiched between the patients with appointments.

Phyllis knew most patients by sight if not by name, another reminder of the closeness of this country community. It made Maddy feel alien, lonely, apprehensive, rather as she had yesterday when she'd arrived and met the ghastly Mrs Gumbrill and the politely cool Dr Trellawney.

An image sprang into her mind, not of the doctor with the frosty stare but of the man with the sad, haunted eyes.

She stamped on it and concentrated on work, but she couldn't shake off the feeling of being an outsider. Everyone she'd met had been pleasant enough, but how did they see her—as a foreigner, someone to be wary of?

Certainly Mrs Cathy Malone, arriving for a regular blood test, viewed her with deep suspicion.

'No offence meant,' she said, meaning it with every glance, as Maddy sat her down and asked her to roll up her sleeve, 'but Phyllis had better do this. She knows my funny veins.' She kept her sleeve firmly rolled down.

'She's busy with another patient,' explained Maddy.

'Then I'll wait.'

Inwardly fuming, Maddy tried a friendly smile. 'I have done this before, Mrs Malone, many times.'

'Not on my veins you haven't,' replied Mrs Malone.

Phyllis sang out from the other cubicle. 'I'm going to be a while yet, Cathy. Best let Sister Coleman get on with it. She's from a busy London hospital and, believe me, has seen loads of funny veins.'

'London!' snorted Mrs Malone. 'It's not the be all and end all.'

'True,' said Maddy, 'or I wouldn't be here.'

Her conciliatory response surprised Mrs Malone. She stared hard at Maddy, then slowly began to roll up her sleeve. 'Oh, well, in for a penny, in for a pound,' she ground out reluctantly. 'You'd better have a go.'

She *did* have difficult veins, flaccid and hard to find but not impossible. Maddy tightened the restricting band, tapped up the almost invisible blood vessel and smoothly inserted the needle. Got it in one.

It was over quickly. She withdrew the needle, released the band and fixed a small dressing over the puncture point. 'All done, Mrs Malone.'

Mrs Malone rolled down her sleeve. 'I just hope I

don't have a bruise,' she said as, with Maddy's help, she shrugged herself into her coat.

'So do I,' agreed Maddy, crossing her fingers behind her back as Mrs Malone marched out of the treatment room.

A few minutes later Phyllis showed her patient out and Maddy said cuttingly, 'Thanks for dropping me into that one.'

Phyllis grinned. 'Had to happen some time and I've done you a favour. My eyes aren't what they were. I'm not brilliant at doing bloods and you obviously are. Mark my words, she'll be asking for you next time.'

'I should be so lucky.'

'Anyway, don't mind her—she's a crony of Mrs Gumbrill's.'

'Oh, that accounts for it,' said Maddy with a laugh.

Toward the end of the morning Dr Trellawney phoned— he was sending in a Mrs Runnicorn for an electrocardiogram.

'You or Phyllis, fit her in stat,' he said tersely to Madeleine. 'And send her back to me with the read-out.'

'Certainly, Doctor,' she said calmly, but a wave of indignation swept over her. Did he have to be so damned brisk? She glared at the receiver and was about to replace it when he added softly. 'And she needs reassuring. She's a very anxious, very sick little lady and needs a bit of the old T.L.C.'

Her indignation disappeared in a flash. She was glad that he obviously cared. She said softly, 'Of course. Will do.'

'Poor old Mary Runnicorn,' said Phyllis a few minutes later when Madeleine relayed the message. 'She's not been looking well. Not surprised if her heart's a bit dicky the way she slaves away on the farm, and that son of hers does damn all.' She frowned. 'Look,

Maddy, you do the ECG. She's proud, rather prudish, may be a bit embarrassed if I do it—I think she'd prefer a stranger.'

'Of course. I'll go and get things ready.'

The ECG machine was in the room next door to the general treatment room, and while Madeleine's hands were busy with leads and receptors her mind was busy, too.

She was touched by Phyllis's thoughtfulness and the doctor's concern, which he'd expressed with reluctance—as if afraid to admit that he cared as a man as well as a doctor. There was nothing wrong in that—admirable, in fact.

Or was it part of a veneer with which he protected himself, as she'd suspected yesterday? The more she thought about it the more convinced she became that it was exactly that, and that beneath the veneer was another more vulnerable, much warmer man.

There had been a glimpse of it last night when he'd told her about the injured tractor driver, and again this morning, speaking of the new baby. And of course there was that occasional smile. There was nothing cold about that. Both Phyllis and Karen obviously admired him, thought him kind and a super doctor. So why was there sometimes a wintry expression in those grey eyes? And why the distant manner that he seemed to turn on and off at will?

There was a knock at the door—Mary Runnicorn had arrived. The questions, at least for now, would have to be shelved. Perhaps she would never know why, but she resolved, as she had last night, that she would do her utmost to find the answer. Almost against her will, Dr Trellawney intrigued her.

It took some time to reassure Mrs Runnicorn, a little sparrow of a woman, and help her remove several layers of woolly vests, jumpers and cardigans, and then explain in layman's language what an electrocardiogram was and how it worked.

'This machine records through these leads and discs how your heart is working,' Madeleine said, positioning the discs on the thin, bony chest. 'The findings are printed out on a strip of paper in the form of a graph, which will give Dr Trellawney the information he needs to decide what treatment to give you.'

'I won't have to go into hospital will I, Sister?' Mrs Runnicorn asked, adding in a voice that she was obviously struggling to keep steady, 'You see, I can't leave the farm.'

'I don't know, Mrs Runnicorn,' replied Madeleine gently but truthfully. 'It will be up to the doctor, but he'll only send you into hospital if it's absolutely necessary—you can be sure of that.'

She had no doubt that he would do just that when she saw the read-out, spilling from the machine a few minutes later—the graph was zig-zagging madly all over the place. She didn't consider herself an expert, simply an informed observer, but if ever a heart needed stabilising this one did.

She said as much to Phyllis when she returned to the treatment room.

'Good,' snapped Phyllis fiercely, to her surprise. 'Of course I'm desperately sorry it's so bad, but the best thing that could happen to her is a spell in hospital, a complete rest. That'll make Mervyn pull his finger out— he'll have to if the farm's not to go under.'

'But will he do that? Perhaps he'll just let things slide, and that won't help his mother, lying in bed worrying about what's going on. Just what a heart subject needs— anxiety.'

'Mervyn won't let that happen,' said Phyllis firmly. 'He loves his mother, though he takes advantage of her.

It'll give him the fright of his life when he knows that she is really ill. He'll buckle to.'

'But will he realise how ill she is? Mrs Runnicorn strikes me as the sort of person who keeps her woes to herself. Bet she plays it down to him.'

'Then we must make sure that doesn't happen,' said Phyllis. 'We'll have a word with Dr Trellawney—get him to put the fear of God into Mervyn.'

'Will he do that?'

'Like a shot, if he thinks it will help his patient. We'll have a word with him later.'

'Later' was just before lunch when the centre closed from one till two.

'Right,' said Phyllis, after they'd cleared up the treatment room, 'let's go and put the boss in the picture about Mary Runnicorn.'

'Do you need me along?' Maddy asked. For some unaccountable, irrational reason she was reluctant to come face to face with the man who had been resident in her thoughts for most of the morning.

Phyllis looked at her in surprise. 'Of course you must come along—you did the ECG, talked to Mary, are concerned for her. Believe me, he'll appreciate whatever you've got to say. Besides, he'll want to know how you got on this morning.'

'Oh, right. And how do *you* think I got on this morning? I felt pretty lost at times.'

'Well, it certainly didn't show. I think we've got the makings of a good team, you and I. I just hope you don't get bored with our slow rustic ways after life in the big city.'

'I won't,' replied Maddy, suddenly confident that at least workwise she would fit in to this Cornish village. There would be something very satisfying about getting to know the patients and following their treatment through. 'Thanks for making me so welcome.'

'A pleasure, and I mean that—not just as a figure of speech. Now, let's go beard the lion.'

The lion had just finished making a phone call when, in answer to his staccato reply to their knock, they entered his office.

'I'm glad you're here,' he greeted them, as he cradled the receiver. 'I want a word about Mrs Runnicorn.'

'Bingo,' said Phyllis. 'That's precisely why we're here. We're worried about her.'

He frowned. 'So am I. I want to admit her to the Royal and she's virtually agreed, though very reluctantly. I think she's frightened—not of going into hospital but for some other reason. Something's bothering her badly, and if either of you have any idea what it might be, please, put me in the picture. She completely clammed up on me.'

Dr Trellawney looked from one to the other, his face set and serious. 'I need to know if she's likely to back out of going into hospital. She's hovering on the brink of a coronary, and it's imperative that I get her to go in. Who did her ECG?'

'I did,' said Maddy.

His wide mouth turned down at the corners. 'Made grim reading, didn't it?' Probing, questioning eyes met hers over rimless half-spectacles, sitting on the high straight bridge of his nose.

She ignored the little disconcerting flutter in her chest. 'It did—it was all over the place. She must have been feeling ghastly, but she seemed more worried about leaving her farm than her own condition. But Phyllis can fill you in about that.'

'Ah, the fount of all local knowledge.' He swivelled sideways to face Phyllis, who had perched herself on the edge of the examination couch. He gave her a little half smile. 'OK, Phyllis, give—tell me why our nice and, I would judge, normally sensible Mrs Runnicorn is so up-tight?'

'Because of her lazy, spoilt son, Mervyn,' replied Phyllis promptly, and repeated what she had told Madeleine earlier.

'And you think that if I put him squarely in the picture, regarding his mother's condition, he'll face up to it and pull himself together—give her the support she needs?'

'Yes. He loves his mother and as long as you make him understand how ill she is he'll take care of her. Basically, he's a good son, but he cracked up when his father died—it coincided with him being jilted by his girlfriend. Mary spoilt him rotten, and since then he's just sat back and let her get on with managing the farm which, though small, is damned hard work.'

He said grimly, 'Right, then, I'd better get weaving and do something about it.' He picked up the phone. 'I'll have a word with our Mervyn. I want that woman in hospital this afternoon. Thanks for your help, ladies. Let's hope it pays off for our patient.' With a nod and a faint smile to accompany this cool praise, he dismissed them.

As they reached the door he said, 'By the way, Madeleine, how are you settling in—finding us a bit dull and tame after St Kits?'

Pleasure shafted through her. He was interested, as Phyllis had said he would be. She turned and beamed across the room.

'Different, but certainly not dull or tame. Stimulating, in fact.'

He looked almost surprised. 'Oh, really! Great! Let's hope that you will continue to feel that way.' On this somewhat cryptic, doubtful note he turned back to the phone and began to punch in a number.

'Well,' said Madeleine as they closed the door behind them, 'what was all that about?'

'That's our Stewart, being a bit tongue-in-cheek,' said Phyllis.

'Don't you mean sarcastic?' replied Madeleine acidly.

She felt bruised as well as angry. He'd practically implied that she wouldn't last the course, almost, she thought, as if he didn't want her to. But that was nonsense—why on earth shouldn't he?

Phyllis shook her head. 'No, he wasn't being sarcastic. I think he was trying to say that he hoped you approved the set-up and would be happy to stay with us.'

'Then why on earth couldn't he say so?'

'It's not his way.' Phyllis shrugged. 'He tends to be reserved, except with patients, especially with women— unless they're prim old spinsters like me. But don't let it bother you. You'll get used to it.'

But would she? Madeleine wondered at intervals as the busy day wore on.

How could she work happily with a man who apparently had two sides to his nature, a man who could be thoughtful and considerate or stiff and almost taciturn? A man, honesty compelled her to admit, who attracted her in a peculiar off-beat way, although she'd known him for barely twenty-four hours. She was bewildered.

Nothing like this had happened to her since she'd started her training and had been dotty about a fifth-year medical student. He'd made her heart turn cartwheels and her pulses jump like crazy, but then she had been seventeen, going on eighteen. Now she was twenty-seven, going on twenty-eight. The doctor didn't have quite that effect on her, but he certainly *did* something to her.

It really isn't on, she told herself wryly. Women of my age just don't allow themselves to be bowled over by any man, especially by a man with a mysterious past and some sort of hang-up about women. So pull yourself together or pack the job in! Can't do that, she reminded herself. I'm committed for three months. Time enough to come to terms with Stewart Trellawney, or time to admit that she'd made a ghastly mistake and return to London!

Meanwhile, play it as cool, as he does.

With relief, tinged with regret, she learned that they were unlikely to see any more of the doctor that day. It would give her some breathing space.

'He's doing visits to the outlying villages this afternoon, and is holding a fit man's clinic this evening, which he manages on his own,' explained Phyllis.

They both went off duty at five, Phyllis to the home she shared with her elderly mother a few streets away from the centre and Madeleine to the village stores a few hundred yards down on the other side of Pilgrim Street to top up on her groceries.

The self-service stores were surprisingly well stocked, though some items were a bit pricey. But the vegetables were cheap and very fresh. 'Local produce,' said an assistant, who was filling a tray with fat round sprouts.

Madeleine was drooling over the cheese display when the woman behind the counter suggested, 'Why don't you try a bit of Yarg, Sister? It's a pure Cornish cheese made nearby—lovely.'

Madeleine looked up in surprise at being addressed as Sister as her uniform was concealed beneath a thick quilted jacket. There was something vaguely familiar about the smiling face opposite... Then recognition dawned—the varicose ulcer she'd dressed this morning. She dredged up a name from memory.

'It's Mrs Jerome,' she recalled. 'I didn't recognise you at first in your white overalls.'

'Well, you did see more of my leg than the rest of me,' said Mrs Jerome with a chuckle.

'True...' Madeleine smiled. 'This Yarg—is it really good?'

'Smashing, it's half solid, half soft. Have a taster.' She cut off a generous sliver and speared it with a cocktail stick.

It was mouth-watering—whitish, pale, creamy.

'Mmm...very nice. I'll have just over a quarter of that, and a half of mature Cheddar, please. I'm what you might call a cheeseaholic,' she said ruefully. 'I just can't resist a good cheese.'

'Believe me, there are worse things to be hooked on than cheese, Sister,' said Mrs Jerome, as she wrapped and labelled the two wedges. Maddy thought the smile disappeared for a millisecond, but decided that she was mistaken when Mrs Jerome said cheerfully, 'Goodnight,' and added, 'I'll let you look at my ulcer again next week, Sister.'

'I can't wait,' laughed Madeleine, as she crossed to the checkout.

Being recognised by the friendly Mrs Jerome had given her a warm glow, and it was with a light heart that she made her way back to the centre through the snowy sludge of Pilgrim Street. Perhaps after all, in spite of the wariness shown by some of the patients and Stewart Trellawney's reserve, she might, in time, find herself being accepted in St Kellier's.

It started to snow again as she turned into the court-yard, and with her head down she dodged around the parked cars and sprinted towards the staircase up to her flat. She was brought up short when she bumped into the solid frame of the doctor as he was crossing from The Old House to the surgical block.

'Oh...so sorry,' she murmured breathlessly, rocking a

little as she blinked up at him through the whirling snowflakes.

He took hold of her shoulders to steady her. 'Are you all right?' he growled.

Funny how a mellow voice like his could growl! She inhaled deeply. 'Fine, thanks.' She shifted the laden carrier bag from one cold hand to the other.

'Here, let me,' he said, and, taking her by surprise, firmly removed the bag from her frozen fingers and strode off in the direction of the iron steps.

Madeleine hurried in his wake—like the page in 'Good King Wenceslaus', she giggled helplessly in her head. 'There really isn't any need,' she gasped as she caught up with him.

'There is. It weighs a ton, and the steps are still as slippery as last night.' He paused at the foot of the staircase. 'You go ahead and open the door.'

It was useless to argue.

He was on her heels as she stumbled up the steps, and stood behind her as she fumbled the key into the lock with icy fingers.

'You should have worn gloves,' he said flatly, 'and a hat or something.'

'I know, eighty per cent of body heat is lost through the scalp.'

The door was open at last. She switched on the light. He stepped past her, brushing against her as he did so. She shivered.

'You're freezing,' he said, dumping the carrier bag on the worktop, as he had last night. He turned round and took hold of her hands and began rubbing them gently. 'Got any whisky in the house?'

'No...but I've got some plum brandy.'

'One of the exotic items from your friend, Fee?'

'Yes.'

'Have half a glass—warm—then something to eat.' It was an order.

'Will do.'

He let go of her hands and moved to the door. 'By the way, Mrs Runnicorn is safely installed in the Royal.'

'Oh, I am glad.'

'So am I, and relieved.' He stepped out onto the snowy platform. 'Goodnight, see you in the morning.' He closed the door softly but firmly and she heard him scrunch down the steps.

Unheard, she whispered goodnight to his downward-retreating form—for the second time in twenty-four hours.

CHAPTER FOUR

OVER the course of the next few days, Maddy met most of the staff at the centre. They were busy days, with a constant stream of patients to be attended to, though there were occasional lulls.

It was during a lull on Thursday afternoon that one of the receptionists, Joy Rivers, rang the treatment room to report that an elderly man had just arrived in Reception, with blood streaming from his nose.

'It's absolutely pouring out. Don't know him—he's a visitor, staying with Olive Tregowan who keeps a B and B. She's brought him in. Can you deal with him, or shall I get the duty doctor to see him when he's free?'

'I'm free now so I'll come and fetch him. Sounds as if he needs some attention as soon as possible. What's his name?'

'Sidney Black.'

'Let's see if we can make you more comfortable, Mr Black,' Maddy said, as she sat the man down in a curtained-off corner of the spacious treatment room. Tall and thin, he was bleeding profusely from his long, pointed nose. 'Are you subject to nose-bleeds?' she asked.

'No,' he mumbled, through a soggy handful of tissues.

She disposed of the soaked tissues, tilted his head over a bowl and instructed him to breathe through his mouth as she gently pinched his lower nostrils together. She took his pulse with her other hand. It was sluggish, slightly fluttery.

Ten minutes later he was still bleeding. She phoned Stewart Trellawney, the afternoon's duty doctor. Her heart did a little flip when he picked up the receiver.

'Dr Trellawney, it's Madeleine Coleman. I've got a severe, right-sided epistaxis, bleeding like a stuck pig, shows no sign of easing up,' she murmured, so that neither her patient nor the one that Phyllis was attending in the other cubicle would overhear. 'I'm concerned. He's an elderly man, a Mr Black. I think it may be a sealing-off job. He's looking a bit washed out and his pulse is feeble and erratic.'

'Right, have everything at the ready for plugging or cauterising. I'll be with you shortly,' he replied.

Nice of him to accept my assessment without question, Maddy thought as she helped her patient from chair to couch and explained that Dr Trellawney was coming to have a look at him.

Mr Black protested feebly, 'Don't want to be a nuisance. Don't need a doctor, it's only a nose-bleed.'

'The bleeding's been going on rather long, Mr Black. You might need a little more than simple first aid to stop it,' she said.

Stewart arrived as she finished laying up the trolley. His eyes swept over the forceps, nasal plugs, swabs, receivers, anaesthetising agent, surgical gloves, head torch and the electro-coagulation probe unit.

He nodded. 'Of course—all present and *very* correct, as I would expect.'

Sarcasm! No! Teasing, perhaps. His mouth curved into a smile—a kindly one, warm and sincere.

Maddy felt her breathing quicken—because of a smile? Ridiculous!

She said evenly, 'This is Mr Black, Doctor. As you can see, he's still bleeding profusely.'

Stewart patted Mr Black's shoulder. 'Yes, you are, aren't you, old chap? I'll just take a look and see what needs to be done to stop it.' He pulled on surgical gloves, put on the head torch and bent to examine the heavily bleeding nostril, swabbing away what blood he could as he did so. After a moment he straightened.

'It's going to be a cauterising job, Mr Black,' he explained. 'Uncomfortable, but not painful. I'll numb your nose before I start but you'll have to keep your head back while I seal off the bleeding point. You'll feel the blood running down into your throat but we'll keep it mopped out so that you don't choke. The whole procedure will only take a few minutes. Sister will get you organised.'

Maddy clipped a paper towel around the patient's neck and lowered the back of the couch by several inches.

'All right, Doctor?' she asked.

He nodded as he perched himself on a stool near the head of the couch. 'Fine, thank you, Sister.'

They worked deftly together. Maddy constantly mopped up the steady stream of blood, draining into the patient's throat, and murmured reassuringly as Stewart anaesthetised the right nasal passage.

There was a pause as they waited for the local to work. Then, with steady fingers, Dr Trellawney carefully introduced the needle-like rod, conducting the high-frequency electrical current, into the nostril.

'Try to breathe outwards as I do this,' he instructed. There was a faint hum from the transformer as he switched on the current and pressed the needle against the bleeding point. After a moment he withdrew the probe, adjusted his head lamp and peered into the nostril. 'One more go,' he said, 'should do the trick.'

He repeated the procedure and, after another brief examination, gave the all clear. 'All done, Mr Black. I'll let Sister sort you out.'

Mr Black coughed and spluttered and spat into the

bowl that Maddy held beneath his chin. Maddy swabbed out his mouth for the last time as the blood, dribbling down his throat, eased to a trickle.

She offered him a handful of clean tissues, but warned, 'Dab, but don't blow. Continue to breathe through your mouth for a little longer and keep the pressure off your nose.'

'I'll try,' mumbled the old gentleman, closing his eyes and slumping back against the pillows.

Stewart put a hand on his shoulder. 'Well done,' he said reassuringly. 'You're going to feel a bit shaky for a while so please stay put—we need to keep an eye on you. I think a milky, sweet cup of tea and a biscuit are in order, don't you, Sister?' He raised an eyebrow and slanted a smile across at Maddy.

Maddy nodded, 'Definitely, Doctor.' Tea and sympathy, a time-honoured method to reassure and rally a mildly shocked patient. She looked down at Mr Black. 'Well, Mr Black, do you fancy a cuppa?'

Mr Black opened one eye. There was almost a twinkle in it. 'Don't take sugar,' he croaked with a grimace.

Stewart patted his shoulder. 'Consider it medicine,' he said.

'OK…and thanks for everything, Doctor.' He opened his other pale blue eye, and looked from Stewart to Maddy. 'You and Sister here. Thought you might think me a bit of a fraud, coming in with just a nose-bleed. I'd have been given short shrift at home, that's if I could have got an appointment at all.'

'We aim to please.' Stewart grinned. Gently he squeezed the patient's papery-thin old hand in his strong, lean one. 'Well, goodbye, Mr Black, take care. Your nose is going to be a bit painful when the analgesic wears off but a couple of paracetamol should put that right. Come back if you have any problems.' And, with a polite nod of thanks to Maddy, he whisked himself out of the cubicle.

He's always walking away from me, thought Maddy crossly, eyeing the billowing curtain. It was a ludicrous thought. She pulled herself together and concentrated on clearing the trolley.

'Nice bloke,' said Mr Black. 'Human, like.'

'Very,' agreed Maddy, sounding as laconic as Phyllis and wishing with all her heart that she could be as laid-back as her sensible, down-to-earth colleague.

Or think of Stewart Trellawney simply as a nice bloke, she thought as she made her way to the staffroom to make tea for her patient.

It was a wish that remained with her for the rest of the day and which she took to bed with her that night, but there was no way she could emulate Phyllis's philo-sophical attitude. She lay awake for a long time, trying to sort out her jumbled thoughts. Why, she asked herself for the umpteenth time, does Stewart Trellawney have this peculiar effect on me?

OK, he's good-looking and, from what I've seen so far, he's a top-notch doctor, but I've known plenty of men who fit that category, who are neither spiky nor as reserved as he is, and they didn't turn me on. Turn me on! *Not true.* She sat bolt upright in bed. Crude, yucky phrase—and, of course, it wasn't true. She was a mature woman. She didn't get 'turned on'—that was for teen-agers.

She tried to organise her thoughts. Can't pretend that I don't find him attractive, but it's nothing more than that. It's because he's such an enigma, frosty one minute and friendly the next. He intrigues me, has done from the word go. In spite of his coolness, something sparked between us just briefly when we first met and he lowered his guard, revealed his vulnerability.

According to Phyllis, something in his past makes him wary of women. But what? If she doesn't know, is there anyone who does? Mike Roach, perhaps, or Alison Peachey, or maybe Karen Foster, the mother hen? Or was the old doctor, Dr Marric, whom Stewart obviously admired, the only person privy to his mysterious past?

In which case, I'll never know unless he tells me himself and, short of a miracle, that's not very likely. He'll go on hugging his hurt, disillusionment, whatever, to himself.

Perhaps it's just as well. I came down here to sort myself out, get off the treadmill, decide what I want to do with my future—not get mixed up with a mixed-up man. The best thing I can do if I'm to come to terms with the peculiar effect Stewart Trellawney has on me is to keep my distance from him or convince him that I only want to be a friend. Neither will be easy.

And on this sombre thought she eventually snuggled down under the duvet and fell asleep.

She didn't see anything of the doctor on Friday. He was away all day, apparently at a meeting with the local health authority in Penruth.

To her annoyance, Maddy was acutely conscious of his absence. In a few short days she had grown accustomed to hearing his voice in the corridor or catching glimpses of him in Reception. Just knowing he was around was reassuring, and today he wasn't and she missed him.

So it was with relief that she went off to assist Alison Peachey in the children's asthma clinic in the afternoon. It would be something new to get her teeth into.

She and Alison had already established a liking for each other and worked smoothly together throughout the session. She was surprised by the number of children who attended the clinic and the range of sophisticated machinery available for testing their respiratory efficiency.

'I'm amazed,' she said to Alison, when the busy session ended and they were enjoying a well-earned cup of tea, 'that there are so many kids suffering from asthma here in the country, with all this fresh air and no pollution to speak of. How come?'

'Well, asthma is increasing among children all over the country, and the extrinsic factors, like house mites and fur and feather allergens, are the same everywhere. And this is farming country—quite a number of children develop animal- and crop-related allergies, usually mild and easily contained with the right treatment in the early stages or, better still, by taking preventative measures.'

'Hence all the testing equipment.'

'Yes, we've a strong policy on prophylactic medicine and it pays dividends. We pick up some very early signs of asthma and are able to treat accordingly. We encourage adults or children to come for tests if they show any signs of the disease—you know, breathlessness, wheezing, dry cough, tight chest.'

'You've got some super state-of-the-art stuff here—it must have cost a bomb. I'm surprised your funding would run to it.'

'It wouldn't. It came out of money old Dr Marric left in trust for the practice. The partners and Karen and our accountant are trustees and vote on how to use it, but anyone can make suggestions—staff or patients. This was our first major project, but there are all sorts of ideas in the pipeline. It's by no means straightforward. Every penny has to be accounted for and cleared with the authorities.'

'And to think that I left Kits under the impression that I was leaving all this talk of finance behind me. How naïve can you get?' said Maddy drily.

'Happens everywhere now, juggling with funds.

Stewart's a wizard at it. Don't know how he fits it all in and copes with his list as well but, then, he's single-minded, a workaholic and hasn't anything or anyone to distract him, poor man.'

Maddy's skin prickled with anticipation. At last she was going to find out something about the enigmatic doctor. 'What do you mean—"poor man"?'

'Metaphorically speaking, he seems emotionally drained. I don't think he's got over his wife's death, though that was about four years ago before he moved down here from Glasgow. Perhaps he never will. I've come to the conclusion that he's either that rare animal, a one-woman guy, or he simply hasn't met another woman who appeals to him.'

The news that Stewart was a widower, and a still-grieving one at that, threw Maddy off balance for a moment. She said wryly, 'Well, he's not likely to meet her, living the sort of monkish lifestyle you've depicted, is he?'

Alison shook her head. 'No, and it's not for want of invitations. A handsome man on his own—he has plenty of those.' Her eyes twinkling, she grinned broadly. 'He'd be quite a catch for anyone who could break through that iron reserve, don't you think, Maddy?'

Maddy breathed in sharply. The inference was plain. It was almost as if Alison had read her thoughts, knew how much Stewart Trellawney intrigued and attracted her and was suggesting in a teasing sort of way... That idea must be squashed at once. It must be treated as a joke.

She laughed. 'If you're suggesting what I think you are, Alison, forget it. I hardly know the man and, any-way—'

'There's someone else?'

It was tempting to invent a lover, working overseas, for whom she was waiting. It would soon filter through to Stewart and make him less wary of her, perhaps even encourage him to be friendly, but she couldn't do it. It would be cheating and much too complicated, not her style.

She met Alison's eyes boldly. 'No, there's no one else. I'm a free agent and I like it that way, no ties, no commitment— except to my work—and I've never met anyone who's made me feel differently.' *Until now*, whispered a disconcerting, traitorous little voice in the back of her head.

'I know what you mean,' replied Alison. Her voice was soft.

'Neither had I until about a year ago when I met Roger—it was immediate for both of us.' Her eyes danced. 'You know, across a crowded room stuff, only in this case it was across a highly strung mare, giving birth to a large foal.'

'Well, it's different,' said Maddy. 'How come?'

'I was visiting a friend who kept stables and I was called in to lend a hand, fetching and carrying. Roger was the attending vet, up to his elbows in blood and guts. Our eyes met and…well, that was it, just like the song says. Roger bought into a practice down here and we were married a couple of months ago.'

She stood and began to stuff odds and ends into her medical case. 'Believe me, Maddy, it can happen to anyone at any time, any place. I'm all of thirty-two and it happened to me.'

It flashed through Maddy's mind that a few days before she herself would have said it couldn't happen to her—now she wasn't sure. She wasn't sure about anything, except that Dr Trellawney drew her like a magnet, and she now knew why he sometimes had that haunted look—he was still in love with his dead wife!

Anyway, it took two to bring about love at first sight, as had happened to Alison and Roger, and so far there wasn't the least sign that Stewart saw her as anything more than a useful addition to the practice. And she wasn't even sure what it was she felt for him. Not the kind of love that Alison was talking about, more a feeling of wanting to understand and share the pain that she'd seen in his eyes on that first afternoon.

'What did Stewart's wife die of?' she asked abruptly, as Alison snapped her case shut.

'Cervical cancer...' Alison pulled a face '...though he never talks about it so I know no details. But I'm pretty sure that's why he's so very hot on tests—smears, mammograms, testicular investigations, whatever.' She glanced at her watch. 'I'm off. I'm cooking something special tonight—it's Roger's birthday and he's promised to be home early, that is if he's not doing something unspeakable to one of his four-legged patients.'

She crossed to the door. 'It's been great working with you, Maddy, and...forgive me for being pushy but, about Stewart, don't be afraid to go for it. He's a nice guy, you know, beneath that reserved exterior.' She opened the door and said with a grin, 'All he needs is the love of a good woman—bye, see you.'

'Oh, go home to your man,' said Madeleine, with an answering grin.

She sat and stared into space for a few minutes after Alison had gone, then, her mind busily churning over the conversation they'd just had, mechanically began to tidy up the clinic room.

She was putting the last piece of equipment away when the door was opened abruptly and, to her surprise, she turned to find Mrs Gumbrill in the doorway, dragging a vacuum-cleaner behind her. She bit back the suggestion that the housekeeper might have knocked and said politely, 'You obviously want to vacuum around. I won't be a moment.'

Mrs Gumbrill's black eyes were just as hostile as they

had been on her arrival a few days before. 'Thought the room was empty,' she muttered through tight lips. 'Clinic's usually done by now.'

I'm damned if I'm going to apologise to the old witch for not being finished, thought Maddy. She locked the cupboard door, gathered up notes and folders and marched angrily out into the corridor, saying coolly, 'It's all yours, Mrs Gumbrill.'

'Don't let her get to you,' advised Phyllis, when, still fuming, Maddy arrived back in the treatment room. 'She's an evil old thing and would have been burnt at the stake a couple of hundred years ago.'

'I don't know why or how Stewart Trellawney puts up with her,' said Maddy.

'Because he feels honour-bound to keep her on. She sort of goes with The Old House, though I suppose he could get rid of her if he wanted to. But he won't do that—he's too kind.' Phyllis began to unpin her cap as she walked to the door. 'Well, I'm off. Thanks for doing tomorrow morning, my first Saturday off for yonks. Have a good weekend.'

'Will do,' replied Maddy, outwardly cheerful but inwardly rather dreading her first weekend alone in St Kellier's.

Saturday morning would be all right. The centre would be open from eight-thirty to eleven, and Stewart would be on duty— her heart gave a little bump of pleasure at the thought—but after that she would be on her own. The surgery would be empty except for the possible occasional coming and going of Mike Roach, the on-call doctor.

It hadn't really sunk in until now that for the first time in years she wouldn't be spending her weekend tending bashed-up football supporters or, off duty, partying or clubbing or going to the cinema. And she would miss seeing Fee or Naomi, though she'd be phoning them to let them know how her first week had gone.

That was something to look forward to. There was plenty to tell them—she'd give them potted descriptions of her colleagues. The laconic, likeable Phyllis, Karen, the kindly mother hen, the besotted Alison, the ghastly Mrs Gumbrill and, of course, the enigmatic Stewart Trellawney.

She'd mentioned him on Monday night when she'd rung to confirm that she'd arrived safely, and they'd been intrigued to learn that he was not the ancient old doctor of their imagination. They'd certainly want to know more.

What would she tell them? Face to face it would have been possible to talk about her ambivalent feelings towards him, but it would be difficult to convey over the phone. They would think her mad, behaving out of character if she admitted that she was attracted to a man she had only just met. But, then, they'd thought that the whole Cornish venture had been mad.

Maddy dreamed confused, troubled dreams of Stewart Trellawney that night but couldn't remember the substance of them when she woke up, feeling curiously light-headed and washed out through lack of proper sleep. And she looked it, her mirror confirmed when she sat down to apply her make-up a little later.

Well, at least I'm not likely to face Stewart for an hour or so, she comforted herself. He'll be too busy in his surgery first thing.

Wrong! He was the first person she met when she went on duty. He was waiting for her at the foot of the staircase, just as he had on her first morning. His searching grey eyes swept over her pale face and came to rest on her slightly drooping mouth.

'You're tired,' he murmured, his eyes never leaving her mouth.

A picture jumped out at her from the jumbled kaleidoscope of her dreams—his mouth was crushing hers, his teeth nibbling at her lips and licking delicately with the tip of his tongue.

She stiffened and held her breath, and for one wild moment, standing on the stairs in the cold light of morning, she imagined that he could see what she could see. Impossible. It hadn't been *his* dream—he had been in hers.

But her cheeks went crimson at the thought, then the colour drained away, leaving them almost colourless. What else had she dreamed? With an effort she made herself look straight at him and exchange stare for stare.

His long, tender mouth, looking exactly as it had in her dream, curved at the corners in a gentle smile.

'You didn't sleep well,' he stated, his voice soft.

She shook her head and shrugged. 'Not very.'

'You're not worried about holding the fort on your own this morning, are you?'

Was that what he thought?

'Heavens, no.' She conjured up a smile. 'Phyllis is a good teacher and has shown me the ropes. I know where everything is and there are only a few patients booked in for me to see.'

She was babbling, but he seemed not to notice. His eyes still held hers.

'Saturday is usually pretty quiet after the first hour, but don't hesitate to shout if you need help.'

'Will do.' It was an unreal, stilted exchange—he must have known that she was quite able to cope.

'Be sure you do… Oh, by the way, Mrs Runnicorn— remember, the lady with the switchback ECG read-out?'

'I remember, you had her admitted to hospital in Penruth. Have you heard how she's doing?'

'That's what I came to tell you. She's going to have a bypass next week—she's being rested till then. Looks as if we caught her just in time.'

'*You* caught her.'

'It was a team effort.' They smiled at each other—quite suddenly, a relaxed, easy smile. Briefly the tenseness between them disappeared and they were in complete professional accord.

'Thank you.' Maddy glanced at her fob-watch. 'Lord, I'd better get going,' she said, 'or I'll be late for my first patient and have the boss after me.'

Stewart's eyes gleamed. 'Difficult chap, is he, your boss?'

'Very,' said Maddy, and, turning smartly on her heel, marched briskly away from him along the corridor. She was pleased with herself. For once he could look at *her* retreating back.

Her bravado was short-lived and had completely disappeared by the time she reached the treatment room. She felt muddled over the whole episode and acutely embarrassed by the vividly recollected dream. She knew he couldn't possibly know that she had dreamed at all, still less that she had dreamed about him, but she had an uncomfortable feeling that somehow he'd guessed. The vibes between them had been so strong—or had she imagined them?

She needed time to mull over what had occurred between them during their curious conversation, a conversation full of undercurrents. But now was not the time or the place to mull over anything. She had work to do.

Her first patient, Tony Loder, was a large lad of sixteen who was booked in for the removal of stitches from a gashed knee. Stitching of a flesh wound was unusual these days, but a note in Phyllis's handwriting explained that Tony was allergic to medicated glue. It happened occasionally. The wound was almost healed. The edges had knitted well except for one small spot, and Maddy had no hesitation in removing all but three of the neat stitches.

'I want these three stitches to stay in for a few more days, Tony,' she explained, as she secured a dry dressing over the wound with a firm Tubigrip knee bandage. 'Come back on Wednesday and I'll see if they're ready to come out. Till then, don't overdo it with that leg— give it a chance to heal.'

The lad looked at her in dismay. 'Does that mean that I can't play rugger this afternoon?'

'It certainly does, though surely that would be impossible anyway—the fields are still covered in snow, and there's more forecast.'

'Go on, a little snow wouldn't stop me.'

'But your leg will unless you want to end up with a real problem,' Maddy said firmly. 'Off you go, and make an appointment to see me on Wednesday.'

'I don't believe this,' grumbled Tony. 'You sure I can't play?'

'Positive.'

He glowered at her and limped out of the room, banging the door behind him. Maddy filled in his treatment card and went through to the waiting room to collect her next patient, Mr Ted Bennett.

Mr Bennett had been booked in to have his ears syringed.

'I've bin putting in the drops to soften up the wax, like Sister Taylor told me,' he shouted, as Maddy sat him down and tucked a paper towel round his neck.

'Good,' Maddy mouthed back at him. 'That's a great help.'

It took some time to evacuate the accumulated wax of a lifetime from the old gentleman's ears. It was a common but skilled procedure that had to be done slowly in order not to damage the eardrums or upset the balance as hearing was gradually restored.

'How does that feel?' she asked, when she had removed the last plug of wax and mopped up the residual moisture and debris.

Mr Bennett stared at her, his eyes wide with surprise. 'I can hear you,' he said, 'as clear as a bell. Thanks, Sister, it'll be a treat to be able to enjoy the telly again.'

The next patient was Mrs Jane Burden, a woman of forty who was in for a cervical smear. Because she had been at work, she hadn't been able to attend the mid-week cervical session. A slim, good-looking woman, she'd had twins and two other children in quick succession in her early twenties but had not to date had a smear done.

'Any particular reason for deciding to have one done now?' asked Maddy.

'I've just moved here and registered with the practice. I read your leaflet in the patient information pack that I was given about how important it is to have a regular smear. And it's so easy, not having to see the doctor but booking straight in with the nurse.'

'That's the idea,' said Maddy, who had herself been impressed by the information pack that was issued to all patients and which, she'd learned from Phyllis, had been introduced by Dr Trellawney.

The smear didn't take long to do, though the patient had a first-degree prolapse which slightly narrowed the entry into the cervix. When she had finished, Maddy mentioned it to Mrs Burden. 'Does it worry you at all?'

'Not a bit. Didn't know I had a prolapse—why, is it dangerous?'

'No, but if it drops a bit further it might be uncomfortable. Mightn't be a bad idea get it looked at by one of the doctors.'

'I'll think about it.'

'Fair enough. Give me a ring in about ten days' time. The results of the smear should be back by then.'

Her next two patients were quickly dealt with.

The first was an elderly, elegant but obese lady who came in weekly for her weight to be checked. She was thrilled to bits when she found that she'd lost another kilogram.

'What's that in proper English?' she wanted to know.

'Just over two pounds,' said Maddy, marking her chart.

'Marvellous!' beamed Mrs Moor, 'Dr Trellawney said I could do it if I stuck to his diet. That's seven pounds in three weeks.'

'Congratulations,' said Maddy. 'See you next week.'

Her last patient, Alan Lloyd, was a smart, middle-aged man, going to the Far East on a business trip, who had come for his anti-tropical diseases jab. He'd had many such jabs over the years and was familiar with the procedure so was in and out in a few minutes.

The phone rang as Mr Lloyd disappeared through the door. It was Stewart, brisk and professional—vastly different from the gentle, honey-voiced man of a couple of hours earlier.

'Sister, I'm sending along a Carol Clarke, thirteen. She's had a fall, query a badly sprained or fractured right wrist. Please fix her up with a strong support bandage and a plastic cuff. Make it safe for travelling. Mrs Clarke's with her and is taking her into Penruth for an X-ray.'

Maddy matched his briskness. 'Will do, Doctor.' There was a knock at the door. 'I think they've arrived,' she said, adding, as she was about to replace the receiver, 'And I think a full elbow sling might be in order, don't you, Doctor? Make it more comfortable as well as safe.' She couldn't resist overdoing the professional bit.

He chuckled. 'Good idea, *Sister*,' he said.

It was half past ten when Maddy finished with Carol, who was very stoic though clearly in a lot of pain. 'But that's much better,' she said, when Maddy gently eased her arm into the sling that supported her whole hand and encased her elbow.

'Keep it close to your body,' advised Maddy.

'OK, and thanks, Sister.'

'Yes, thank you,' said Mrs Clarke, rather grudgingly, Maddy thought. Mrs Clarke looked round the treatment room. 'Phyllis off, then, today, is she?'

Oh, no, not another of Mrs Gumbrill's resentful cronies, thought Maddy. 'Yes,' she replied shortly.

'Hmm,' said Mrs Clarke. 'Well, we'd better get going if we're to make it to the hospital before we get snowed in. Come on, Carol.'

CHAPTER FIVE

MADDY pottered around after the Clarkes had gone, clearing up the treatment room and entering the morning's written notes into the patients' records on the desktop computer. She inspected her watch—eleven o'clock. She went through to the waiting room. It was empty, except for Lorna Smith, the pleasant, middle-aged receptionist.

'Great, no more customers,' said Maddy, relaxing against the desk. 'Anyone in with the good doctor?'

'No,' said Lorna cheerfully, ticking off a list of names in the appointments book against the pile of files in front of her. 'He's actually finished on time for once, and I've locked up so he can't see anyone else.'

'Oh, well, in that case, I'll shut up shop and have an early lunch. I'm going in to explore Penruth this afternoon.'

'And *that*, Sister Coleman, if I may say so,' broke in Stewart from behind her, 'would be a foolish thing to do in that ancient little sardine can of yours in weather like this, especially as you are unfamiliar with the terrain.'

Maddy bristled and went rigid for a moment. How dared he criticise her or Genevieve? She took a deep breath and turned to face him. 'No, you may *not* say so, Dr Trellawney,' she replied in an icy voice. 'What I do in my own time is my own affair.'

Their eyes clashed, grey and tawny, both glittering with anger. 'Not,' said the doctor, 'if it might involve other people in coming to your rescue.'

'And why should they have to do that? My little sar-

67

dine can, as you so contemptuously call it, got me to this God-forsaken place in a snowstorm.'

She heard Lorna mutter, 'God-forsaken. Well, really.' She wished her hasty words unsaid—the last thing she wanted was to offend the friendly receptionist.

She turned her head smartly. 'Sorry, Lorna, I didn't mean to be rude. I haven't seen much of the village yet, but the centre certainly isn't God-forsaken—it's brilliant, and I enjoy working here. It was a slip of the tongue. You can blame the doctor for doubting my driving ability and making me so mad. Am I forgiven?'

Lorna hesitated for a moment, then grinned and shrugged. 'All right, I believe you, though thousands wouldn't. You're forgiven for rubbishing the village that I love.' She picked up a pile of bulging medical records. 'Well, I'm going to file these and leave you two to it. Have fun.' With a wink, she disappeared through the door which led to the filing room behind Reception.

Maddy turned back to face Stewart.

He gave a snort of what sounded like exasperation. 'I was *not*,' he said forcefully, 'doubting your driving ability.'

He suddenly smiled a lopsided smile that lit up his face and emphasised the network of fine lines that radiated from the corners of his eyes.

'I wouldn't dare. I was only pointing out that a small car like yours is not suited to our country lanes in this sort of weather. There's a lot more snow around than there was when you arrived, and more on the way. Though the highway to Penruth is kept clear, the lanes are not, and how the hell do you think I'd feel if you got stuck miles from anywhere and succumbed to hypothermia?'

'Cross?' she asked drily.

'Responsible...and probably pretty shattered.' His

smoky-grey eyes, reflecting his smile, gazed down at her.

Shattered! Would he really be, or was he teasing, trying to placate her? He seemed genuinely sorry that he'd offended her and it had been a nice apology. The expression in his smiling eyes clinched it. Her anger subsided. 'Would you,' she asked, teasing back, 'really be shattered?'

'Yes,' he said, 'I would.'

There was something about the intensity with which he uttered the stark words that gave them a significance which she couldn't fathom—or was she imagining it? Imagined or not, the words hung in the air as they stared intently at each other in silence.

Maddy's breathing quickened. It was shallow and she felt almost faint, conscious that she was hyperventilating. She leaned back against the desk and forced herself to take a few deep breaths, expanding her diaphragm. That was better. She must break the silence, pretend it hadn't happened.

'Well, we can't have you being shattered, Doctor, can we?' she said with a little laugh. 'I'd better give in graciously and promise not to go further than the village today—always supposing that's not out of bounds.'

His body language changed. The tenseness went out of him, and he grinned. 'Not at all,' he said. 'Make the most of the fleshpots of St Kellier's. You know, it's an historic village—tin-mining past, castle ruins on the outskirts and an ancient coaching inn, serving super homemade food. You should try it—I go there occasionally.'

Did he? If only he would ask her to go with him!

She feigned surprise, raised her eyebrows and for once in her life decided to play it coyly, as she'd seen other women do, though she despised herself whilst doing it. 'But wouldn't the locals mind a lone female, and a stranger at that, straying into their pub?' she asked innocently, willing herself not to blush. Pathetic! She wasn't any good at this.

It was Stewart's turn to look surprised. He frowned. 'I wouldn't have thought you nervous of going into a pub on your own.'

She'd blown it, that was for sure. She was hopeless at playing the helpless little woman. 'I'm not nervous exactly, just uncomfortable, feeling very much a stranger in a strange land.' That at least was true. 'Everyone seems to know everyone else and, well, I don't.' That was true, too. Then, in case that sounded too feeble, she added brightly, 'But I dare say, given time, things will improve.'

She fancied that he looked relieved, but couldn't be sure.

'They will, believe me, I know. You'll soon start making friends,' he said.

Maddy recalled Alison, saying something along the lines that he was inundated with invitations.

It's all right for him, she thought, not knowing whether to be bitter or sad, but I'm just a spare female. Who's going to bother with me? Oh, stop feeling so sorry for yourself, she told herself impatiently.

He said softly, 'I wish—' Abruptly he stopped, then went on, 'Look, Madeleine, I must go. I've a couple of visits to make and an appointment to keep. I won't be back till late tomorrow night.' He touched her arm. 'It won't bother you, will it, being here in the building on your own?'

He was away for the weekend. Her heart plummeted but she forced a smile. 'No, of course not. I'm used to living on my own. Have a good weekend.'

'Thanks. See you Monday.' He called through to Lorna, who was still in the filing room. 'Goodbye, Lorna. Have a good weekend.'

'Will do, and you.'

Stewart hovered, seeming reluctant to move. Maddy kept the smile pinned on her face.

'Go on,' she said, 'or you'll never get away.'

'You sure you'll be all right?' he said. His eyes were kind, his voice gentle. She wanted to cry, or be held in his arms and feel that wide, tender mouth...

What the hell? She swallowed. 'Fine. I told you, I'm used to living on my own.'

But not, she realised, back in her flat a little later, with no one living above or below her. The silence was not quite absolute. She could hear the snow-muffled rumble of traffic on Pilgrim Street, but within the building it was deathly quiet and it *felt* empty. In her London flat she had always been conscious of people being around, even if she couldn't actually hear them.

She looked out of the sitting-room window. The staff car park was empty. Every vehicle had gone, including Stewart's tough Land Rover which stood outside The Old House most of the time—a comforting reminder that he was around. Always at the ready, it was seldom garaged until late at night, and not even then if he was on call. Even Genevieve wasn't there. She was tucked away safely in the converted stables at the end of the courtyard, which served as garages.

For the first time in her adult life Maddy was truly alone, and the temptation to bawl her head off was tremendous. This wouldn't do.

'Coleman, get hold of yourself,' she said loudly, then added mentally to herself, OK, so you're on your own—tough. You wanted to change your lifestyle, and you have so get on with it. You're working with a nice bunch of people, Phyllis, Alison, Karen, and, given time, you'll get to make friends with them off duty and you'll start socialising as you did at Kits.

And what about Stewart Trellawney? nagged a little voice. Do you seriously want to start socialising with him, become his friend? Are you simply attracted to him because he's such an unknown quantity, alternately aloof or warm, self-assured or vulnerable? Forget the peculiar effect he has on you, that's purely physical, just body chemistry—do you really want to have to cope with a relationship that could be fraught with problems from the outset?

Yes! shouted the voice, loud and clear in her head, *I do*!

Relief washed over her like a tidal wave. She'd reached a momentous decision and she knew exactly what she was going to do. She would take Alison's advice and go for it—make this man her friend and, perhaps, in the fullness of time...

'Nothing ventured, nothing gained,' she could hear her late, beloved foster-mother say firmly.

Well, she would venture.

Suddenly she didn't feel lonely any more, but brimfull of confidence in the future. She switched on the radio and the imitation log fire, made a pot full of fragrant coffee and knocked herself up a herb omelette, which she ate with relish.

It reminded her of the evening of her arrival when she and Stewart had both been ravenously hungry and had tucked into Mrs Gumbrill's delicious tea almost in silence.

He'd looked incredibly handsome in the blue sweater that had softened the steel in his grey eyes. And the firelight had glinted on his jet black hair and flickered on his long fingers as they'd neatly dissected a crumpet, before popping a segment into his wide, tender, buttery mouth. Remembering vividly, her heart skipped a beat.

He had a lovely, vulnerable mouth, a square jaw, strong but gentle fingers and deep-set, intelligent thoughtful eyes that missed nothing and were sometimes stern and uncompromising. It all added up to a very masculine, caring man of integrity.

Maddy sighed with pleasure—that was the message that had come over loud and clear in the short time she had worked at the centre. Her decision was right. It would be worth even risking a rebuff to get to know the man behind the reserve. She would work at it.

Feeling rather light-headed, as well as light-hearted, she set out after lunch to explore St Kellier's. Snow began to fall again as she sallied forth down a surprisingly busy Pilgrim Street but, stylishly booted and swaddled in a padded thigh-length jacket over woollen tights, the cold wind, driving the snow before it, didn't bother her. But it proved Stewart's point that crossing the moors in gallant little Genevieve would have been mad.

It was after four o'clock and almost dark when Maddy returned to the flat. The orange carriage lamps, which came on automatically as the light faded, cheerful and welcoming, lit up the car park.

'Home sweet home,' she muttered, as she lugged her full carrier bags carefully up the snowy steps, and with the words came the realisation that it was the first time that she had thought of it as home, not just as the flat.

The phone started ringing as she entered the warm kitchen. She dumped the shopping and reached for the receiver. 'Hi,' she said breathlessly, not bothering to give her number—knowing it would be Fee or Naomi.

'Would I be right in thinking that you've been struggling up those damned steps again with a load of shopping?' said Stewart Trellawney in her ear.

Her fingers tightened round the receiver. Already breathless, she became more so and her voice came out as a whispery squeak. 'Well…yes.' She must pull herself together. Her nostrils flared with the effort of taking a deep breath. She cleared her throat with a raspy cough and said, in a crisp, cutting voice, 'Why, is that also on the list of things I'm forbidden to do, Doctor?'

A deep chuckle came over the phone. 'As I said earlier, I wouldn't dare to forbid you anything, Madeleine, but allow me to be concerned. Those steps are lethal at the moment and you do tend to take them at a run.'

'Thank you for being concerned but, you know, I am a reasonably fit and healthy woman not yet in her dotage, well able to climb a few stairs unaided.'

'I know, two at a time with those...' he hesitated slightly '...long legs of yours but, just the same, take care.'

So he'd noticed her legs! And she was almost sure that he had been about to say 'lovely' or 'super' before 'legs', as most men would have done but, then, he was not most men and not given to fulsome compliments.

She almost purred with pleasure, but made herself say calmly, 'I will. But did you ring for any special reason— want me to contact a patient or look up something in the records?' Though why he should want to do that when he was off duty she couldn't imagine.

'No, there's no other reason. I just wanted to make sure that you're all right. It seems hardly fair that you should be on your own on your first weekend with us.'

Her heart thundered against her ribs. 'We've been through all that,' she said softly, 'but I really don't mind, you know. Please don't worry about me.'

After a short pause, he said, 'Right, I'll try not to. Goodnight.'

'Goodnight.'

Slowly she hung up the receiver, and heard the click of his phone a fraction of a second before hers.

She stood motionless beside the phone, breathing hard. 'I'll try not to,' he'd said, as if it wouldn't be easy. Did he mean that he couldn't help worrying about her?

Or did it just mean that he felt responsible for her as an employee? Perhaps it didn't matter either way. This reserved, private man cared enough to phone—that was what mattered.

Still bemused by the intense pleasure that his call had given, and the enigma that was Stewart Trellawney, she was draping her damp jacket over a radiator when the phone rang again. This time it had to be Fee or Naomi. It was both of them, speaking from Fee's house.

'I'm on the extension in the bedroom,' Fee explained. 'Naomi's downstairs.'

'Hi,' said Naomi. 'We've been deserted by our menfolk, both away at conferences, so we're having a girls-together weekend. Personally I think these conferences are just an excuse for them to junket around, chatting up those glam female medics.'

Perhaps that was where Stewart had gone—to a conference, Maddy thought.

'Speak for yourself,' cut in Fee. 'I know my man—he only has eyes for me, disgustingly gross as I am with his child. Anyway, enough about us. I want to know about you, Maddy. How are things at the end of the world? Bet you're pining for the bright lights already. It must be ghastly on your own.'

'But I'm not on my own,' retorted Maddy. 'I'm working with a nice bunch of people, the centre's much bigger and busier than I imagined and the equipment's first class—I haven't come across a single rusty scalpel to date.'

'Oh, good... But when you're not working,' Fee persisted, 'what on earth do you do with yourself?' It was as if she wanted to find a flaw.

'Well, today's been the first day I've been off in daylight, and I've been exploring the village.'

Both of them snorted with laughter.

'Bet that took all of five minutes,' said Naomi.

'Actually,' replied Maddy airily, 'it took me all afternoon. Pilgrim Street, that's the main road, may not be Oxford Street but it's got everything from a small classy boutique to a delicatessen. And I had a mouth-watering, real Cornish pasty in a quaint old place called The Tea Parlour, tucked away in a cobbled lane off Pilgrim Street, and—'

Fee butted in. 'OK, we get the message, we're convinced—St Kellier's isn't exactly off the map, but don't you miss the big city, and us, just a tiny bit?' She was almost pleading.

'Oh, Fee, of course I do, and until this morning I wanted to bawl my head off every time I thought of you both.' She knew as soon as she'd spoken that it had been the wrong thing to say.

Naomi was onto it at once. 'So the million-dollar question is what happened this morning to bring about this miraculous change? I'm intrigued. Come on, Maddy, you can tell us.'

Madeleine clutched the phone hard—could she? Yes, of course. She wanted to confide in them, try to put them in the picture about Stewart Trellawney and the effect he'd had on her from their first meeting. She wanted to explain what a complicated man he was, strong but vulnerable, and how this morning had climaxed with her decision to break through his reserve. But she hesitated, not having a clue how to begin.

Naomi broke the small silence. 'It's something to do with your new boss, the dishy doctor you mentioned the other evening, isn't it?'

How did she know that? 'Yes, it is, but I didn't say he was dishy, did I?' She couldn't really remember what she'd said that first evening because she'd been tired and disorientated.

'You said he wasn't old and was presentable and implied that he was dishy.'

'Well, I wouldn't call him dishy exactly—he's too solid and reserved for that—but he's got loads of magnetism, though he doesn't seem to be aware of it. He's a bit of a slave-driver, works himself and everyone hard, but nobody minds and he's awfully good with the patients.'

'You've fallen for him!'

Maddy hesitated fractionally, then said slowly, 'I rather think I have…a bit, but—'

'But?' Naomi and Fee spoke impatiently in unison.

'He has a thing about women.'

'You mean he's—?'

'No, there's something in his past to do with his late wife. According to Alison, our female medic, he puts up this tough front but behind it is terribly vulnerable, and nobody seems to be able to get through to him. I think she's right. He is vulnerable and sad so this morning I made up my mind to—'

'To discover the man beneath the veneer,' interrupted Fee.

'And offer a shoulder to cry on,' supplemented Naomi. 'What else, Maddy being Maddy?'

A shoulder to cry on! How well they knew her. 'It's the least I can do,' she said fiercely. 'I don't know how it'll turn out, but I just know that I've got to try—he's worth it.'

'If that's the way you feel, there's no argument, you should go for it,' said Fee.

'Like a shot,' agreed Naomi. 'No point pussyfooting around.'

They talked a little longer, mostly about the advent of 'little orthopod'—as they'd christened Fee's baby—then, promising to make contact the following weekend, they said their goodbyes and rang off.

Sunday slipped by pleasantly as Maddy waded through the bulky broadsheet that was her favourite newspaper, and performed a few small chores about the flat.

It had stopped snowing some time during the night, and she went for a brisk walk in the pale wintry sunshine after lunch out of the village and up onto the snow-quilted moors. She arrived back at the centre just before dusk to find Mike Roach's car in the courtyard, and the man himself emerging from the surgery.

'Hi.' He beamed her a broad smile. 'Not burgling the place—called in to pick up some notes for an old chap over Rosebourne way, who's had a fall. Sounds a bit iffy and he's one of Stewart's so I've got to be on the ball.'

'Hope you're always that, Mike.'

'Of course, but you know what I mean.' He grinned ruefully. 'It's like being up before the head. He'll give me the third degree in the morning.'

'Don't exaggerate.' Maddy laughed. 'You make him sound like an ogre, and he isn't—he just cares.'

'Ah, so he has yet another admirer. Lucky old Stewart, how does the man do it?' He didn't seem to bear his colleague any animosity. His twinkling blue eyes swept over her. 'Like the fur cap,' he said. 'Very becoming.'

'It's not real fur.'

'I'm glad to hear it.' He stretched out and touched it lightly. 'But it adds to the picture of outdoor freshness—very Russian, very Dr Zhivago, very attractive.'

Beware of his charm, thought Maddy, remembering Phyllis's warning. But he really is rather nice.

She smiled. 'Thank you.'

He unlocked his car door. 'Well, regretfully, I must away—duty calls. See you tomorrow, Maddy. Enjoy the rest of the day.'

'I will.'

The evening dragged a little, though Maddy spent an inordinate amount of time preparing her dinner, a variety of fresh vegetables with roast chicken and an elaborate sauce. She kidded herself that this was because she enjoyed cooking and trying out new recipes but she knew that, in fact, she was killing time until Stewart returned.

She had the television turned low and heard the squeaky screech of tyres on the frozen snow as he stopped outside The Old House. It was nine o'clock. She crossed to the window, parted the curtains a crack and looked down on the well-lit courtyard.

Stewart was climbing out of the car, the rosy lamplight shining on his dark head and giving it a bronzed look. Maddy's heart performed what was fast becoming a familiar flip—it was so good to see him. She felt foolish. He'd been away barely two days and she'd known him only a week, but it seemed an age since they'd parted yesterday morning and since his phone call last evening.

Her hand, holding the curtain, shook a little, and at that moment he looked up. Had he seen the crack of light and realised that she was watching for his return? 'Hell, I hope not,' she muttered, letting the curtain fall into place. Although she had made up her mind to build a relationship, instinct told her to go cautiously, be cool and professional, so that he wouldn't feel his private life threatened.

Yet it surprised and hurt a little when she was summoned to Stewart's office the following morning and he greeted her with an abstracted and rather curt, 'Good morning.' He made no reference at all to his absence or enquired how she had spent her Sunday. She had thought—hoped—that he might.

He was sitting at his desk, frowning over something he was reading, his lightly tanned skin taut over his chiselled cheek-bones and his lips a straight line. He barely gave her a glance as he waved her to a chair. It was difficult to believe that he was the same man who had cared enough to phone on Saturday. Suddenly she understood what Mike had meant about being hauled up before the head.

A shiver of apprehension ran through her. She suppressed it. It was ridiculous to feel nervous—she had nothing to be nervous about.

'Phyllis said you wanted to see me,' she said brightly. 'Am I to have a ticking-off about something?'

He looked up from the letter in his hand and transferred his frown to her. 'No of course not. Whatever gave you that idea?' he asked in an astonished voice, uncreasing his eyebrows and lifting one expressively.

'You looked rather grim and forbidding,' said Maddy, her eyes very bright as she stared at him boldly.

His eyes glinted in return, a faint smile touching the corners of his mouth. 'Letters from the health authority usually make me feel grim.'

She smiled back. 'I can imagine. I'm glad it has nothing to do with me.'

'My dear Madeleine, every communication emanating from the powers that be affects everyone eventually.' His voice was as dry as dust.

'Oh, I suppose it does.' She wished she could think of something more intelligent to say. 'Can I help?'

'Yes, by continuing as you've begun. You're a first-class nurse, an asset to the practice, and we're lucky to have you. Phyllis is singing your praises, and Alison is delighted with the way you coped in the asthma clinic— says you have a way with the kids.'

She laughed. 'To tell you the truth, I was a bit overwhelmed at first—so many of them together. They tend to come in in dribs and drabs on A and E. And they're usually pretty sick or injured, not like Alison's youngsters who, in spite of their asthma, were mostly so well and boisterous.'

'Alison's a wizard at balancing medication, which is half the battle with controlling the disease.'

'Yes, and she's marvellous at persuading the children to co-operate, even the smallies. I was very impressed.'

'Do you like working with children?'

'Yes, I thought at one time about specialising in paediatrics.'

'Did you, indeed?' He smiled. 'So you won't mind helping me out with my kids' clinic this afternoon?'

'Love to.' Her voice came out breathily. The prospect of working with him all the afternoon made her pulses race.

'Good. We start at two so open up a bit before and bring the records with you. Reception will have them ready. Phyllis will fill you in on the routine.' He nodded toward the door. 'Thank you, Sister, see you anon.'

Sister again! She was dismissed. But even his brusqueness couldn't dent her euphoria that she seemed helpless to control, and she decided that as she couldn't fight it she would enjoy the sensation.

Several mothers and children were queuing outside the clinic room when Madeleine arrived, although it was only twenty to two.

'They're not booked in at certain times,' Phyllis had explained. 'It's a question of first come first served, which means,' she added with a laconic grin, 'that you have to list them in order of arrival and God help you if you get it wrong.'

Maddy groaned. 'No wonder you didn't mind handing it over to me.'

Phyllis chuckled. 'No good getting old if you don't get artful.'

Stewart arrived bang on two, ruffling hair and greeting many of the children by name as he waded through the sea of noisy little ones towards the office at the end of the room.

Over their heads he smiled at Madeleine, who was sitting at the table a little way from the door, listing patients as they arrived.

'Bit like a rugby scrum, isn't it?' he said in a raised voice. His eyes, bright with amusement, crinkled at the corners. She had never seen him so relaxed. Her heart did a sort of double flip. 'You'd better come through and brief me on the order of play,' he added, and went on, over his shoulder as she got up and followed him, nursing a handful of records, 'Have you managed to weigh and measure anyone in yet?'

'The three O'Malley children, the Cundy twins and Andrea Pengilly. They're charted.' She piled the records on the side of his desk.

He beamed at her. 'Well done, you have been busy.' He took off his jacket and draped it over the back of the chair, rolled up his shirtsleeves, loosened his tie and sat down behind the desk. 'The casual look, for the benefit of the kids,' he explained. 'Sorry if I look a bit scruffy, but they seem to find it less daunting.'

Madeleine found herself staring, mesmerised, at his tanned forearms with their smattering of curly black, bronze-tipped hairs. She hardly heard him, but registered the gist of what he was saying.

She looked up to find his eyes fixed on her face. Willing herself not to blush, she floundered, 'Scruffy. No, of course you don't look scruffy—you should see some of the medics I've worked with.'

'Mostly youngsters fresh out of med school, hell-bent on looking world-weary and streetwise,' he guessed. 'We've all been through that phase, haven't we?'

'Yes, though it seems to have got worse over the last few years.'

'I've noticed.' He gave a smothered snort of laughter.

'Lord, listen to us. We're like a couple of old-timers—nothing is as good as it was in our day.'

'Well, it isn't,' she said stubbornly. 'Student nurses don't look like student nurses any more. They don't wear uniforms, and the present training system only allows them to observe. They don't do any hands-on nursing.'

He nodded. 'So I believe.' His eyes travelled over her face, seeming to examine it in close detail. 'It really bothers you, doesn't it?'

'Yes.'

'You must tell me about it some time.' His voice was quiet, sincere.

Her heart stood still. Could this be the beginning of friendship? 'I'd like that,' she said simply.

'Good, we'll fix something soon.' He picked up the top buff envelope and smiled up at her. A warm current flowed between them. 'Now, wheel in the O'Malley brood and let's make a start,' he said softly.

Feeling quietly jubilant, Madeleine sailed through the afternoon.

She weighed and measured and gave injections into small arms and bottoms, murmuring reassurances—though not always successfully.

Stewart examined, diagnosed and prescribed. As his hands, large in comparison to the small chests and abdomens he was examining, gently pressed and probed, he listened through his stethoscope. Madeleine was impressed. She had worked with many doctors, good and bad, and recognised an artist at work. A physician who had once lectured her had described the art of examining as 'seeing through one's fingers and ears'.

Which was precisely what Stewart was doing as he looked into the middle distance and concentrated on what he was feeling and hearing.

An uncanny quiet descended when the clinic came to an end at four-thirty. Madeleine said goodbye to the last small patient and gazed around the waiting room. It looked like a battlefield, with toys and books littering the floor.

Stewart came to the door of the office and stretched his sinewy arms high above his head. 'Lord, that was some session,' he drawled tiredly. He looked round the room and pulled a face. 'Do a deal with you, Maddy. You conjure us up tea and I'll give you a hand, tidying up.'

Madeleine caught her breath—he'd never called her Maddy before. She cleared her throat. 'Deal.' She smiled. 'I'll fetch it from the staffroom.'

The phone rang in the office. 'Better hang on,' he said. 'Might be another customer for us, coming up from Reception.'

She began to collect the toys as she waited.

A couple of minutes later Stewart came out of the office, rolling down his shirtsleeves, his jacket slung round his shoulders. 'Sorry, deal's off. A young chap on the Pen Farm Estate, where they raise rare breeds, has been gored by a pedigree bull. I'll have to go... Afraid I'll have to leave you with this mess to clear up.'

She swallowed her disappointment. Tea tête-à-tête would have been wonderful. 'Gored by a bull! The mind boggles. Sounds like yours will be a much worse mess to clear up. I can't begin to imagine what that might be like or what sort of injury might occur.'

'Rather like being hit by an express train armed with knives, I should think.'

'You don't know?'

'No, this is my first experience of a goring. They don't happen that often—with artificial insemination, there aren't many bulls around. I just hope I can do something useful for the poor devil before the ambulance arrives.'

'You will,' she said confidently.

'Thanks.'

Maddy returned to the office, after tidying the clinic room, and worked flat out to put the written records on computer, though her thoughts occasionally strayed to Stewart and his bull-gored casualty.

It was six o'clock by the time she'd finished. Mike had left at five-thirty, leaving her to lock up behind Mrs Tasker, the cleaning lady. She would file the records, see Mrs Tasker off and take herself up to the flat for a well-earned cup of tea and a long mull over the day's events. There was plenty to think about.

She made her way along the deserted corridor to the filing room. It was very quiet, with no noise coming from Reception where Mrs Tasker usually finished her cleaning. There was no sign of her either in the waiting room or Reception. She must still be working at the other end of the building, yet everywhere looked clean and tidy.

Strange! A faint sound came from behind the almost closed door of the filing room. Mrs Tasker? There was nothing to do in there except vacuum. The tightly packed shelves of records were the responsibility of the receptionists. Maddy found herself almost stealthily slipping round behind the polished counter and quietly pushing open the door.

The vacuum-cleaner was there and the cleaning lady was there, but it wasn't the lanky Mrs Tasker but the dumpy Mrs Gumbrill. She was standing side-on to the door and, lips moving silently, was totally absorbed in reading a treatment card that she had obviously extracted from the buff envelope she held in her left hand.

She was quite unaware that she was being observed.

CHAPTER SIX

'WHAT the hell do you think you're doing?' Maddy exploded.

The dumpy little woman seemed to freeze for a moment, then turned slowly, drew herself up to her full insignificant height, lifted her head and regarded Maddy with unwinking black eyes.

'Just putting this back where it belongs,' Mrs Gumbrill said, registering surprise at being questioned. She slid the card back into the wallet. 'I found it on the floor when I came in to clean. It must have fallen out when the receptionist was putting it away.'

'You were reading it!'

'Only to see the name so I could put it in the right envelope.' The sloe-black eyes continued to meet Maddy's, without wavering.

The sheer nerve of the woman! Maddy almost ground her teeth. 'And you found the right wallet without difficulty.' She let her eyes flicker over the tightly packed shelves and come to rest on the second shelf from the top, where a couple of envelopes were half-pulled out. The little step stool was positioned below them.

There was a moment's hesitation. 'That's right.'

'And you thought it was worth climbing up on the stool and searching for the right envelope just to replace a card that could have been handed in when you'd finished work or left under the counter for the receptionists to deal with tomorrow?'

'Yes,' she said defiantly, but there was a wary look in her eyes and for the first time they wavered.

Maddy stared at her in silence. She didn't believe the

woman for one minute, and Mrs Gumbrill knew it. It was virtually impossible for whoever had filed the records not to have noticed and retrieved a card on the floor when she'd descended the steps.

Mrs Gumbrill was lying. For reasons of her own she was interested in the particular medical file that she was still holding, and she had gone to some physical effort to get it. But to prove it, if it came to proving it, was another matter. It would be her word against this malicious old woman's—the newcomer against a long-term employee who, however unpopular, had presumably always been trusted.

Even Phyllis and Alison, with whom she had already formed a rapport, might be inclined to accept Mrs Gumbrill's version of events. Surely not! And Stewart— who would he choose to believe? He would know that Maddy wouldn't lie, but would he think that she might have been mistaken—that the record card had been on the floor—and give his housekeeper the benefit of the doubt?

Of course, he wouldn't have to make a decision if the incident wasn't reported. Did he need to know? Should she keep it to herself? After all, Mrs Gumbrill had had a shock and was surely unlikely to do such a thing again for fear of being discovered a second time.

Maddy broke the heavy silence, and moved across the room. 'I'll take that,' she said, removing the envelope from the older woman's unresisting fingers.

Mrs Gumbrill said defiantly, 'I suppose you're going to report me to the doctor, but I can tell you he won't believe you. He knows the old doctor would've taken my word and he'll do the same.'

'Don't bank on it,' said Maddy coldly. 'You've committed a breach of confidence which he can't easily overlook. Now you'd better go.'

Having seen a bristling Mrs Gumbrill off the premises

in stony silence and locked up behind her, Madeleine slowly climbed the stairs to her flat, made herself tea and sat down to sort out the problem.

If only the wicked old woman hadn't made that final jibe, or had apologised for what had happened, she might have been prepared to overlook the incident with a warning. But everything about Mrs Gumbrill's attitude made that impossible. She wasn't a bit penitent and Maddy felt sure that a warning from her would be ignored. And supposing that something like this had happened before!

Reluctantly, she reached her decision. She would have to report the matter to Stewart, but not tonight. The courtyard was empty so unless he'd been in and out again whilst she'd been busy in her office he hadn't yet returned from his emergency call to the farm. He'd been gone nearly two hours. What sort of mess had he had to deal with there?

She wished she had offered to go with him. She might have been able to help—apply pressure to an artery, give an injection, reassure the victim. But he hadn't asked her, and she was virtually ignorant about first-aiding without the back-up of high-tech hospital facilities and knew nothing whatsoever about dealing with the injuries that an animal had caused.

For a moment her blood ran cold. Supposing the bull was still on the loose and Stewart was attacked, gored like the patient he had gone to attend! Common sense told her that there was no danger of that—the bull would have been restrained immediately after the man had been injured. She was letting her imagination run away with her.

Stewart was not in any danger. He was simply battling, probably against the odds, to save a man's life. His only fear would be that he would lose his patient before he could get him hospitalised, and that—as she knew from personal experience—after fighting for a life, was devastating.

It certainly put the problem of Mrs Gumbrill into perspective. Her breaking of the rules regarding patient confidentiality was serious and would have to be dealt with, but there was no urgency about it—it would keep till some time tomorrow.

What had happened out at Pen Farm was vastly more important. This, rather than the unpleasantness with the housekeeper, occupied Maddy's mind as she prepared supper.

She heard Stewart arrive back soon after seven, and it was with difficulty that she stopped herself rushing down to find out what had happened at the farm. It was out of the question. He would be tired, his clothes bloody, perhaps, and would want nothing so much as a shower and food. Her questions would have to wait until morning.

She was awake early and finishing breakfast when she saw Stewart, crossing the courtyard. She slammed her mug down on the table and her stomach muscles clenched as she hurried down the stairs to meet him.

She waylaid him at the staff entrance. 'The emergency—how did it go?' she asked, touching his arm as her eyes searched his face.

His eyes were bleak. He looked tired, drawn, defeated. She guessed what he was going to say before he uttered a word—it was written all over him.

'He died as we were getting him into the ambulance. He'd lost too much blood and was in shock. Horrific injuries, as bad as any RTA that I've seen. He'd been tossed as well as gored. Did what I could, but it wasn't enough.' His voice was flat, dismissive, and he started to walk with long strides towards his office.

Maddy almost had to run to keep up with him. He

needed to talk to someone who understood and could empathise, though he might not want to admit it right now. But she knew from her own experience the adrenaline-filled motivation that spurred doctors and nurses on to save a life and the sheer hell that followed when they lost a patient. Sharing that experience could help.

He unlocked the door of his office and Maddy followed him in. He raised an eyebrow at her as he shrugged himself out of his coat.

'I don't need anyone to hold my hand, Sister. Patients have died on me before and, in the natural scheme of things, will do so again.'

She ignored the tone of his voice and his hard eyes. 'It can help to talk,' she said gently.

'"It can help to talk,"' he mimicked savagely, and the drawn look on his face seemed to intensify, accenting the lines between nostrils and mouth and hooding his already deep-set eyes.

Her antennae quivered. There was more to this accident than professional immolation—the feeling that one had failed a patient and was inadequate. It went deeper even than that—this was something that affected him *personally*. He *must* be persuaded to talk or it would haunt him for a long time to come—too long. For a man who cared as much as he did it would fester like a boil.

She had to try to find the right words to break through his reserve.

'I can understand you not wanting to discuss it right now,' she said, deliberately keeping her voice even, impersonal, 'but perhaps later.' She turned toward the door.

'No, don't go.'

Maddy turned back.

He stared at her as if he was trying to bring her into focus. A shadow passed across his already drawn face, then he suddenly ground out in a low, cracked voice, 'He was only a kid, sixteen, comes to my teenagers' clinic occasionally, I gave him a character reference for his CV. Keen to work to help his mum out, only just started on the farm. Shouldn't have been in the bull's enclosure.'

He paused, clenching his fists until his knuckles gleamed whitely. 'It was grim, his abdomen ripped open as if he'd been bayonetted, and his mother arrived while I was working on him. I'll never forget the look on her face. Usually so cheerful. We saw her this afternoon—Mrs Cundy, with the twins. Poor woman, she was only widowed last year and now this.'

He spread out his hands, palms uppermost, in a hopeless sort of gesture, his voice dropping further to a throaty whisper. 'Bloody hell when something like this happens. It makes one wonder if there's any point in going on—one can do so little. I honestly didn't know where to start for a minute or two—couldn't believe he was still alive, but he was.'

The urge to touch Stewart was strong, but instinct told Maddy that to overdo the sympathy would be wrong at this point. He needed to—had to—face what had happened, not indulge in self-recriminations.

'Stiffening the sinews,' her foster-mum would have called it.

She said with gentle firmness, 'A familiar story, Stewart. We all feel like that at times but we always carry on, do something, however hopeless it looks, and that's precisely what you did.'

'Tried.'

'Of course you did, and I can see that it must be terribly hard for you to come to terms with the boy's death, knowing him and his family. I suppose it's the downside of this sort of practice, knowing the people involved when something like this happens or you have bad news to impart. But I'm damned sure Mrs Cundy was glad that it was you and not a stranger who was with him at the end. It must be a great comfort to her to know that you were there to do everything you could for him.'

'But did I? If only—'

'Of course you did,' broke in Maddy briskly. 'That's something else we always say—"if only"—when we lose a patient. Stewart, you're a doctor, a very good one, but you're not a miracle-worker.'

'You can say that again,' he said grimly, but his expression lightened fractionally.

Maddy looked at her watch. 'Look, I must go now. Phyllis will be wondering where I am. We've got a heavy list this morning and so have you so you'd better get cracking. Believe me, you may have a poor opinion of yourself, but there are plenty of people out there who have faith in you.'

He took her hands in his and squeezed them hard. His eyes, smoky-dark, met hers. She thought they didn't look quite so desolate.

'Thanks,' he said throatily, 'for bearing with me, not giving up on me when I was so incredibly rude just now, and for making me spill it all out. You're quite right, I'd forgotten how comforting, how necessary, it is to talk to someone who understands, someone who doesn't let me get maudlin or full of self-pity.'

Did he mean his late wife? Had she been a doctor, a nurse? God, how he must miss her even after all this time. Was there a ghost of a chance that he would let anyone else get close to him, fill the void that she'd left?

Her heart went out to him. Tread carefully, don't get too heavy, play it cool, she warned herself. She pulled her hands from his and said quietly, casually, 'Well, I'm almost always around. You can chat me up any time.' Then she spoilt it by blushing like a schoolgirl at what he might see as an innuendo. She took a deep breath. 'What I mean is...'

'I think I know what you mean, Maddy. You're a kind

and generous woman, offering me an ear.' His voice was very gentle.

'Something like that,' she murmured, willing the blush to subside.

She moved towards the door. Stewart beat her to it and opened it wide, and the woody, wholly male scent with which she associated him twitched at her nostrils as she made to slip past him. He put his hands on her shoulders, turned her slowly to face him and looked directly into her eyes. 'I might even take you up on that offer,' he said, and, bending his head, pressed his lips, cool and firm, against her forehead.

It wasn't exactly a kiss, more a friendly gesture—almost like the sealing of a bargain—but quite unexpected, an astonishing thing to come from this reserved man, even in his present vulnerable state. She forced herself not to draw back or show that she was surprised or in any way affected.

'Any time,' she said and, sliding from beneath his hands, walked, outwardly calm but inwardly churning, down the long corridor.

Making a supreme effort, Maddy almost managed to put this emotive, tender interlude with Stewart out of her mind as she concentrated on attending to the continuous stream of patients, arriving for treatment.

Inevitably, everyone wanted to talk about the accident and express their sympathy for the Cundy family. All except Mr Rook. He seemed more intent on apportioning blame than expressing concern for Mrs Cundy.

'Damned silly thing to do, sending a lad of that age to see to a bull,' he said, as Madeleine was changing the purulent, smelly dressings on his stubbornly infected bunions.

'As I understand it, he wasn't sent into the enclosure,' she explained. 'Nobody seems to know what he was doing there. Perhaps they will find out at the inquest.'

Mr Rook snorted. 'Probably find he was up to no good. He's been a right young tearaway since his dad died. But, then, what do you expect—a lone woman, trying to keep a boy like that in line? Women are silly creatures. They need a man around to keep them in order, they're not capable of managing on their own—no brains.'

The old man stared at Madeleine with contemptuous black eyes that reminded her of Mrs Gumbrill's when she had confronted her yesterday. She didn't reply, but swallowed her anger at the frank sexism of his remarks, gave him his antibiotic injection with her usual skill and with a sigh of relief sent him on his way.

Could he be a relative of the beastly old housekeeper? she wondered as she tidied the cubicle.

She would ask Phyllis, and at the same time, perhaps, mention the confrontation she herself had had with Mrs Gumbrill and get her down-to-earth advice on whether or not she should say anything to Stewart—lumber him with yet more problems. She found herself wavering over her decision to report the episode. It seemed trivial in the face of what had happened to the Cundy boy.

'Yes, old man Rook is related to the witch—he's a second cousin,' confirmed Phyllis over coffee. 'Nasty type—mean, sly, always grumbling about something, wouldn't trust him an inch.'

'Sounds like a Gumbrill relative,' said Maddy drily. 'So, would you trust Mrs Gumbrill?'

Phyllis gave her one of her long, shrewd looks. 'Depends in what context. I'm sure she wouldn't pinch anything but—'

'But would she snoop, say at the treatment book, letters or anything like that?'

'Oh, yes,' replied Phyllis without hesitation. 'I'm sure she would, given the chance.'

'And all the staff, including the cleaning ladies, are warned about keeping patient confidentiality, aren't they?'

'They are. Stewart preaches quite a little homily about not repeating anything they may see or hear when they start work in the centre.'

'So Mrs Gumbrill couldn't plead ignorance for reading a patient's records—she would know that what she was doing was against the rules?'

'She would. Why, did you find her going through the records?'

'Yes—well, not exactly going through them.' Maddy explained what had happened the previous evening.

'The wicked old besom. I've no doubt that she deliberately removed those records to read them, but if she sticks to her story it's rather your word against hers.'

Maddy sighed. 'That's my problem, Phyll. You believe me, but will Stewart, if I report it to him, or will he think that I made a mistake or misconstrued what happened?'

'He might, more out of a kind of misplaced sense of honour towards Mrs G than because he really believes her—simply because she's been here since for ever and he feels responsible for her.'

'Because he sort of inherited her from old Dr Marric?'

'Yes.'

'Who, apparently, thought the world of her, though I can't imagine why—she was positively smug about it.'

'Old Dr Marric felt beholden to her for caring for his late wife. She died suddenly of a heart attack, but was in the early stages of Huntington's chorea and getting difficult to manage—beginning to have attacks of dementia. Mrs G was devoted to her, and looked after her until she died.'

Maddy stared at Phyllis for a moment in silence, then said softly, 'Huntington's chorea. No wonder the old boy felt he owed her, and Stewart feels the same.' She shrugged. 'There's not much point in reporting her, is there? As you say, he will feel honour-bound to support her, and I can't say I blame him. What an obligation to inherit.'

'But you *must* report her. You owe it to the other patients, Maddy. Because Mrs Gumbrill was a saint with Mrs Marric doesn't alter the fact that she is a poisonous old mischief-maker from whom the patients need to be protected. Something must be done and Dr Trellawney is the man to do it. How he does it is up to him.' She stood, took her mug over to the sink and washed it under the tap.

Maddy followed suit. 'Yes, I can see you're right,' she agreed reluctantly. 'I just wish it didn't have to be now when he's upset over the Cundy boy.'

'We're all upset over the Cundy boy,' said Phyllis laconically, 'but life goes on, as they say, and we in our profession should understand that better than anyone. Do it, Maddy, tackle him as soon as we finish the list. Catch him before he goes to lunch.'

'Will do,' replied Maddy, making her voice firm and resolute but feeling like marshmallow inside.

With all her heart she wished she hadn't to face Stewart, not only because she didn't know how he was going to react to what she had to say about his house-keeper but because of the way they had parted earlier. Would he be embarrassed, regret that brief kiss that he'd pressed onto her forehead?

High on emotion, it had felt right at the time, but now…

She still felt the same when she knocked at his door an hour later.

'Come,' he called, at his most brusque.

Her heart dropped a notch as she opened the door and

slipped quietly into the room. He was reading something on the computer monitor and, without taking his eyes off the screen which was at a ninety-degree angle to the door, said, 'Take a seat, Madeleine. Won't keep you long.'

How did he know it was her, she wondered, when his back was almost to her and he hadn't even glanced her way?

In part profile, he looked stern and aloof, his high cheek-bones, square chin and powerful nose pronounced in the wintry sunlight, filtering through the blinds, his mouth set in a straight line—a different man from the one she had comforted earlier. This was the strong man on whom everyone in the practice depended.

After a few minutes he switched off the screen and turned to face her, his expression bland and unreadable. There was no sign of his earlier distress—he was in control of his emotions.

Before he could speak she said, 'How did you know it was me when I came in? You didn't look round.' She immediately wished she hadn't spoken and felt her cheeks flush with annoyance. Whatever had made her ask and why on earth was she now blushing?

If Stewart was surprised by her question he didn't show it, but answered without hesitation. 'Your perfume—it's light, delicate, obviously a favourite which you use constantly. I noticed it when we first met, even though it was in competition with the hyacinths.'

'Oh!' He'd remembered that! She couldn't think of anything to say and stared speechlessly at him.

There was a short pause, then he said, 'Well, you did ask.' He grinned suddenly, his eyes crinkled at the corners and his whole face seemed to light up.

Madeleine found herself grinning back. 'So I did,' she said.

'Right, enough of my views on your perfume in the

middle of a working day.' The grin disappeared. 'Tell me what can I do for you, or let me guess—you've come to check up on me to see how I've weathered the morning after my maudlin, unprofessional outburst that you were forced to witness.' His voice was dry, laced again with sarcasm.

Maddy was taken by surprise, shaken by his sudden change of tone and attitude. Obviously he was unhappy at having confided in her. Was he afraid that she would go round boasting about it to all and sundry? Or was he regretting that wretched sexless kiss that he'd planted on her forehead? Or had he so misread her that he thought she would take advantage of that moment of intimacy?

How dared he think such a thing? She must scotch any such idea straight away.

'What do you mean, unprofessional and maudlin?' she rapped out. 'It was nothing of the sort. You needed to talk and, as a colleague, I was ready to listen. I just happened to be there. Anybody else who understood how you were feeling would have done the same, any caring person in the profession. Laypeople seem to think we're as hard as nails and death doesn't touch us but it isn't true, is it, not for most of us? I simply offered constructive sympathy.'

They stared intensely into each other's eyes, Maddy's tawny, amber bright, sparkling with anger, Stewart's at first steel-grey, then gradually shadowing to a smoky blue. After a timeless silence he said slowly, 'You're right, I'm behaving like an idiot. I'm afraid I've grown out of the habit of confiding in anyone. I find it difficult, uncomfortable. Will you accept my apologies and start off from where we were this morning when we seemed to have reached some sort of friendly understanding?'

Maddy couldn't hold on to her anger, didn't want to. She heaved a sigh of relief. 'Yes,' she said. 'I'd like us to be friends.'

Stewart nodded. 'So would I.' He smiled tentatively and her heartbeat galloped. He looked suddenly relaxed, his usual confident self. 'Right.' He sat back in his chair. 'Now we've got that out of the way, down to business. How can I help, Maddy, what's the problem?'

The problem! After the see-saw exchange they had just had, and its satisfactory conclusion, it was going to be even harder to make her accusation against Mrs Gumbrill and perhaps upset the fragile understanding they'd just reached.

'Well, Maddy, what is it? Worried about a patient?'

She shook her head. 'No. I'm afraid Mrs Gumbrill's the problem.'

'Mrs Gumbrill!' His voice was flat, non-comprehending. 'Sorry, you've lost me. Please elucidate.'

She choose her words carefully and gave the plain, unvarnished facts, not commenting on the housekeeper's sly, unpleasant attitude but describing what had happened the previous evening.

He listened to what she had to say without interruption, sitting very straight with his hands linked in front of him and his forearms resting on the arms of the chair.

'Presumably you have discussed this with Phyllis,' he said when she'd finished.

Did he not approve of that? His face was inscrutable.

'Yes, to get her advice. Being the new girl, as it were, I wasn't sure whether you needed to be told. I hoped you wouldn't, but Phyllis thought that you should be put in the picture.'

'She's dead right, the buck stops here. Did you tell Mrs G that you were going to report her?'

'Yes, but I don't think she was impressed.' Madeleine took a deep breath. 'I think she believes she's unassailable and, having heard something of her history, I'm not surprised.'

'Ah, you know about that—how she cared for my predecessor's wife during a stressful illness.'

'Yes, and I can appreciate what a difficult position this puts you in. Look, Stewart, if it's any help, I'm quite happy to forget the whole thing—' The look on his face stopped her.

'No way,' he rasped, 'unless you want to back out because you're not sure of your facts. If you are, you had no option but to report it and I must do something about it. We're talking about patient confidentiality—rule one. I shall get Mrs Gumbrill's side of the story and decide what's to be done. Would you be willing to repeat what you've told me in her presence if she is also willing?'

She had known that it was inevitable, but it hurt that he didn't believe her without question. 'Of course. I don't relish the idea but it's her word against mine and she has every right to challenge me, as I shall her.'

'Right. Will Phyllis be able to manage on her own for a while this afternoon?'

'Yes, it was already planned that she would take the clinic and I would get on with updating files.'

'Then please report back here at two o'clock.' He looked grim and unyielding, but as she stood he said, 'Thank you for telling me, Madeleine. It couldn't have been easy.'

'No, it wasn't,' she replied, letting herself out of his office.

Stewart was alone in his office when she returned at two. Still looking grim, he invited her to sit down.

He said without preamble, 'Mrs Gumbrill refused to come—'

'Really?' muttered Maddy, unable to keep a note of bitter sarcasm out of her voice. 'You do surprise me.'

'But has given me her version of what happened. She

insists that the record card was on the floor and she was returning it to the envelope. Said she tried to explain, but you wouldn't listen.'

'Rubbish! Of course I listened. But it was obvious that a file had been removed from the second to top shelf, a hard climb for someone of Mrs Gumbrill's stature just to return a card to an envelope. And had that card dropped on the floor it would have been noticed. It was also crystal clear that she was reading it and absorbed in what she was reading. I don't want to sound over-dramatic but I would stake my life on it.'

He looked at her steadily for a moment. 'That,' he said drily, 'is what Mrs G said.'

'She would,' said Maddy. 'So you've got to do the Solomon bit and decide whose story to believe.'

'Oh, I know who to believe.' He sounded despondent, weary. 'No contest there...'

'Well?' she asked sharply, leaning forward in her chair.

Stewart frowned. 'Well, what?'

'Not what—who. Whose story do you believe, hers or mine?'

He stared at her in astonishment. 'Why, yours, of course. I've had my doubts about Mrs G often, fancied she listened in to phone calls on the extension, so I wasn't taken entirely by surprise by this incident, though I didn't think she'd go so far as to read records. Oh, my dear Maddy, you don't think for one moment that I was taken in by that nonsense of hers, did you? It was so obviously a cover-up.'

'Well, since you ask, yes, I did think it possible that you might believe her—why not? After all, she's been here a long time and I've only just arrived...' Her voice trailed away.

'Which made it even more unlikely that you would report her unless you were sure of your facts. It would have been in your interest to keep quiet about it, not stir up trouble, especially knowing something of her history and the strength of her position.'

He rose and moved around the desk to stand in front of her. He took her hands in his and pulled her gently to her feet.

'I admire you for putting the patients' welfare first and speaking up. Who knows what mischief Mrs Gumbrill might cause in possession of confidential information? I just hope that this is a one-off and it hasn't happened before. I'm certainly going to make sure that it doesn't happen again.'

'What will you do?'

'I don't know yet. I'll talk to her tomorrow. Leave her to stew a bit, then read her the riot act and put the centre out of bounds—ask Karen to take her off the cleaning roster. There's not much else I can do, short of sacking her.' His wide mouth turned down at the corners in mock horror. 'And no way would I do that and risk one of her curses.'

He drew her slightly closer and said huskily, 'Dear Sister Coleman, what a can of worms your conscience has landed me with.'

Maddy was acutely aware of her hands lying passively in his and the nearness of his body as they stood facing each other, of the masculine scent of him, of their faces only inches apart and his deep, dark, smoky-grey eyes boring into hers, his breath fanning her cheeks. Her pulse raced, her lips parted, seemingly of their own accord, as she leaned closer, her breasts brushing against his chest—

The internal phone rang.

He let out a hissing sigh, muttered something under his breath, gripped her hands hard for a moment, then released them and moved back around the desk to pick up the receiver.

'It'll be my first patient,' he said, his eyes still fixed on hers. 'I asked Reception to let me know when she arrived. I've quite a list to see, before doing my afternoon visits.' He smiled, his eyes very bright.

Maddy smiled back. 'You always have quite a list,' she murmured, her heart pittering and pattering unevenly. 'I'll leave you to it.' She turned at the door. 'When will you finish your visits?'

'Barring emergencies, about six, then I'm on call till midnight.'

'Why not come up for a coffee when you're ready,' she said, willing the breathiness out of her voice, 'and a bite to eat, if you've nothing else planned?'

The phone rang again. He picked up the receiver but covered the mouthpiece. 'I'd liké that,' he said. He turned back to the mouthpiece, and said, 'Yes? Send her in, Joy, I'll see her straight away.'

With a wave, Maddy slipped out into the corridor.

'Well, how did you get on?' Phyllis wanted to know when Maddy arrived back in the treatment room.

'Fine,' said Maddy, and, omitting the intimate moments, gave her a blow-by-blow account of what had taken place between her and Stewart.

'Our Stewart's no fool,' said Phyllis when she'd finished. 'Not surprised he saw through the old witch's story, but I wonder what he's going to do about her?'

'Give her a rocket and warn her away from the surgery block, I believe.'

'She's not going to like that.'

'Tough,' said Maddy, and took herself off to the cupboard-like office to pound away on the computer keyboard for the rest of the afternoon.

CHAPTER SEVEN

MADELEINE switched off the computer at five sharp.

'I'm off,' she announced to Phyllis as she passed through the treatment room.

Already anticipating dinner with Stewart, she felt light and happy, as if she were walking on air. Tonight, she thought, a ripple of excitement coursing through her, could be a breakthrough, the beginning of a friendship with that vulnerable but reserved man who drew her like a magnet. Friendship would be enough for the moment, but perhaps one day...

After the curious highs and lows of the previous week, it was a warming, comforting thought that made her want to hug herself.

'You've got a smile a mile wide,' said Phyllis. 'Like the cat that's got the cream.'

Unable to keep a joyful ring out of her voice, Maddy replied, 'Well, in a way I have.'

Phyllis cocked an eyebrow at her. 'Come on, then, spill the beans. Tell Aunty Phyllis what's put that bloom in your cheeks and that gleam in your eye.'

Why not? She already counted Phyllis as a good friend, and in a roundabout way, because she had insisted that Stewart should be informed about Mrs Gumbrill, had helped bring about tonight's invitation. Phyllis wouldn't think anything of it, except perhaps to be rather pleased that he had agreed to come to dinner—no big deal between colleagues.

She cared about Stewart and, like Alison, had bemoaned the fact that he worked too hard. She had gone out of her way from the start to play down his curtness, making it plain that beneath the spiky veneer was a gentle, generous man and doctor.

As Maddy was dying to share her news with someone, why not with her kind, sensible colleague?

Her smile became even wider. 'Well, emergencies allowing, Stewart's coming to dinner tonight and I must say I'm looking forward to it. He'll be the first person I've entertained in my flat.'

Phyllis positively beamed. 'Well, good for you, old thing. You're over the first hurdle. I was wondering who would make the initial move.'

Maddy's eyebrows shot up in surprise. 'But I don't understand. Make the first move! Oh, no! Are you saying that you guessed that I...? Oh, Phyll, have I been that obvious?'

'Yep. Both you and the boss man.'

'Do you mean...? Are you saying...?' she said raggedly. She swallowed a lump that had mysteriously risen in her throat. 'Phyll, are you suggesting that you think that he—that Stewart—is, well, attracted to me?'

Phyllis's eyes twinkled. 'That's my considered opinion.'

'But how can you tell? He's always so reserved, aloof even. He just doesn't show his feelings.'

Except that he did today, to me, in the office, reminded the familiar small voice in the back of her head, but, then, Phyll doesn't know that, and she still thinks...

A warm sensation flooded through her. It somehow made it more real, a relationship more possible, that even without that knowledge Phyll had detected something between her and Stewart.

'My dear girl, there have been signs to someone who knows him as well as I do. The odd look, a smile, a gesture, his request that you work with him in the paediatric clinic. All this from a man who has hitherto steered clear of any women under forty unless they're firmly committed elsewhere.'

Maddy's stomach churned. So she hadn't imagined the vibes between them. If Phyll could sense them they had to be for real and not a figment of her imagination, which, in spite of the near kiss this morning, she had half feared.

Her voice wavered. 'Are you sure? We've only known each other for just over a week.'

'A day, a week, what the devil's time got to do with it? This thing, call it what you will—love, magnetism, chemistry—can happen in a flash. Believe me, it would be a mistake to ignore it.' Phyll looked up from the dressings trolley which she was dismantling, her usually humorous brown eyes hinting at sadness.

'So go for it, my dear. Let your heart rule your head— you may only get one bite at the cherry. But take it nice and easy at first. Remember he has a lot of lost ground to make up, and that protective veneer of his is pretty thick.'

Her eyes brightened, and she said briskly, 'Well, here endeth the first lesson. Counselling over for today. Just go and enjoy yourself—what are you going to give him to eat?'

Surprised by this sudden change of tack, Maddy said, 'Oh—um—I thought a macaroni cheese—with foil over it, it'll keep hot in a low oven, without drying up, if he's delayed, and then apple pie and custard for pudding. I haven't time to do anything more fancy. Do you think that'll be all right?'

'Made with your own fair hands, he'll think he's imbibing honey and nectar,' said Phyllis in her usual fashion. 'Now scat and get out of that uniform and into something that'll wow him.'

'Well, I don't know if this'll *wow* him,' said Madeleine to her mirrored reflection some time later. 'It's ancient but it's bright and cheerful and *I* like it. It matches my mood.' She sprayed on her favourite perfume, the perfume that he liked, buttoned up the rich multicoloured velvet waistcoat over the wine satin blouse and turned to look at herself side on. She gave a satisfied little grunt.

Ancient it might be, but it did something for her slender figure, emphasising her flat stomach and firm, high breasts. 'Not bad,' she murmured. The stand-up collar of the dark blouse contrasted dramatically with her short, crisp, fair hair and tawny amber eyes, which she experimentally batted at herself.

'You'll do,' she said, and giggled.

She looked at her watch. It was just after half past five—time to get cracking on the food if she was to have it ready for, say, half six or a quarter to seven. By the time he got home, showered and changed, he wasn't likely to show up much before then.

A fleeting vision of Stewart's lean, muscular, soapy body under the shower made her heart bump painfully, her breathing practically stop and the hairs on the back of her neck stand up like feathery antennae. Hair! She *knew* that Stewart would have hair on his chest. Dark and curly, like the scattering of hairs on his arms and the backs of his hands. It would arrow down to his navel and—

She pulled herself up with a jerk and closed her eyes to dismiss the vivid picture. So much for going easy, as Phyll had advised. If she didn't get hold of herself she would throw herself into his arms the moment he stepped over the threshold.

It was a quarter to eight when he arrived.

He shrugged and pulled a face, turning his expressive mouth down in mournful exaggeration when Maddy opened the door to him.

'I can but apologise,' he said. 'I had one call after another.' His breath hung like a cloud in the frosty air.

Maddy's heart skipped a beat or two, but she had herself under control. She gave him a radiant smile. 'So you said when you phoned, but you're here now. Do come in.' She stood aside to let him pass into the warm, aromatic kitchen. Would he kiss her, wouldn't he kiss her? He didn't, but smiled down at her as he slid past. 'Here, let me take your coat,' she offered. 'Food's ready—you must be hungry.'

He sniffed appreciatively. 'Ravenous.' He slipped off his coat and his eyes swept over her as she took it from him. 'You look…stunning,' he said, 'and I haven't even had time to change or shave.' So much for the shower! He stroked his jaw, a shadowy blue-black with a day's growth of beard.

Was it bristly or soft and silky, as she imagined his chest hairs to be? she wondered as she hung his coat up on the rack. She had an urge to touch it to find out. Suppressing a tremor, she turned back to face him.

'Do go through to the sitting room while I dish up, and help yourself to—I thought not wine, as you're on call, but grape juice or low-alcohol lager.'

'Grape juice will be fine. I'm right off anything stronger, even weak lager, having just come from patching up a woman whose drunken lout of a husband has bashed her up,' he said, as he turned and walked through to the sitting room.

Madeleine followed him a minute later, with the steaming dish of golden-brown macaroni.

'Poor woman—was she badly injured?' she asked as she set it down on the table in front of him, adding, 'Do help yourself, and also to salad and rolls.'

'Mmm, thanks, this smells good.' He spooned the cheesy pasta onto his plate.

'So, was she badly beaten up, your patient?'

'Cut over one eye that needed stitching, multiple bruises on arms and legs where he'd knocked her about. Would like to have got her X-rayed, but she refused to go to hospital or inform the police—it was a next-door neighbour who called me. By the time I got there the husband had disappeared, God knows where to. He'll be gone for a few days, then return full of remorse. It's happened before and will, no doubt, happen again.'

'It's amazing how some women put up with that sort of treatment. We used to get them in Casualty. They wouldn't bring charges and the men got away scot-free to do it all over again.' She forked up a mouthful of macaroni and stared at it and then looked across at Stewart. 'Why do they do it?' she asked. 'I certainly wouldn't. I wouldn't protect any man like that.'

His grey eyes met hers steadily. 'You know, you might,' he said softly, 'if you were desperate enough to keep a roof over your kids' heads and keep them fed or…if you loved the guy enough.'

Maddy was speechless for a moment, then spat out angrily, 'I might do it for my kids if it was the only way, but for *love*! No way, I *couldn't* love a man who treated me like that—my pride wouldn't let me. I'd feel cheap, contaminated.'

'You'd be astonished at how many women do stick at it out of love—rise above it, even acquire a kind of dignity. I worked in a rough inner city practice, before coming here, and heard any number of abused women say quite simply, ''But I love him, Doctor, and he needs me.'' And nothing would persuade them to report their partners to the authorities.'

'You almost sound as if you approved of the stand they make.'

'Not a doctor's or a nurse's business to approve or disapprove or get involved. You know that. Strictly speaking, it's our job to do the physical patching up and nothing more—the rest is up to the counsellors and social workers.' He sounded rather brisk, almost dismissive.

'But you don't believe that, do you?' She didn't want him to believe that. She laid her fork on her plate and clasped her hands under her chin. 'I've seen you working, and you *care* about what happens to your patients, don't you?'

He didn't answer at once, but gave her a searching look. Then he said softly, 'Oh, I care, Maddy, have cared, too much, perhaps, for my patients, to the exclusion of...' His voice trailed away and he looked down at his empty plate and fiddled with his fork.

Madeleine stared in silence at his dark head and wondered what was going on inside it. To the exclusion of what? she wanted to ask. Had it anything to do with his sometimes haunted look? Instead she said, 'Your plate's empty. More macaroni, or are you ready for pudding? It's very plain, I'm afraid, just apple pie and custard, not anything as exotic as Mrs Gumbrill produces for you.'

He looked up, his lips curving into a sardonic, lop-sided smile. 'Pudding will be fine. I shall love it.' He paused, his eyes glinting. 'By the way, speaking of Mrs Gumbrill—she's gone.'

Maddy, who was on her way to the kitchen with the dirty plates, stopped abruptly. 'Gone? What do you mean, gone?'

'Handed in her notice, vamoosed, resigned my service, metaphorically packed her bags and returned to her house in the village. Though, to be accurate, she hasn't *lived* in The Old House since Dr Marric died.' His voice was very dry.

Maddy's heart sank. 'But why, why has she gone?' As if she didn't know. His next words confirmed her premonition.

'Because she didn't take kindly to my suggestion that

she steer clear of the surgery block in the future and
stick just to the house. She was positively vitriolic. The
old doctor and Mrs Marric would rise up and strike
me—'

'But that's not fair. You didn't give her the sack. Why
is she taking it out on you? I'm the one who started it
all, I'm sorry to say.'

'Don't be sorry. It was bound to happen some time,
she's been getting more and more difficult lately. And
you won't escape her wrath. I dare say she's sticking
pins into models of both of us right now,' he said with
a wry grin. 'Do you know, I honestly think she believed
that I would send you packing—she was so sure of her
right to be here? I almost feel sorry for her, but there is
a limit to how long one can continue to honour a debt.'

'Especially when it isn't really yours,' muttered
Madeleine through tight lips as she deposited the plates
in the kitchen. She felt both incredibly angry and guilty
on his behalf.

Stewart had followed her and stood in the doorway.

'I wish to God I hadn't— What an unholy mess I've
made of things,' she said, as she loaded a tray with the
pie and dishes and a jug of creamy custard.

'Here, let me take that,' said Stewart, taking the tray
out of her hands. He looked down at her, his eyes a
misty, pearly grey, his voice soft. 'Don't be upset,
Madeleine, you haven't made a mess of anything—just
did what you had to do.' He walked back to the sitting
room and placed the tray on the table.

She followed him slowly and he turned to face her.
'Come here,' he said invitingly, opening his arms wide.

Maddy hesitated a moment, and he repeated, his voice
husky but firm, 'Come!'

Trembling, and with her heart hammering, she stepped
forward and he wrapped his arms round her and held
her close. He smothered the top of her head with kisses,

nuzzling at it so that his warm breath fanned over her scalp. She tilted her head. He kissed her eyelids and trailed his lips down the bridge of her nose to meet her lips. As his mouth closed over hers in a long sighing kiss he whispered, 'Oh, Maddy.'

With a little mew of pleasure she parted her lips and felt his tongue gently probing, circling, exploring the moist interior of her mouth. She nibbled at it, gently at first and then fiercely, almost as if she wanted to eat him or hurt him. She stopped nibbling and murmured against his mouth in a muffled voice, 'Sorry, sorry.'

He lifted his head just a little. 'Don't be.' He raised his head higher. 'What's a little pleasure between friends?'

Friends! What did he mean, friends? And said in that dry, throw-away voice. Surely those tender kisses that he'd just showered on her face and head and that long sexy kiss had been...

Her head spun, she shivered and stared up at him blankly. His lips were curved into a faint smile—mocking? His eyes were still the same soft, pearly grey, but touched now by something else—pain, uncertainty, surprise?

She couldn't read them. Phyllis's words leapt into her mind—'Take it easy at first. Remember he has a lot of lost ground to make up.' She'd gone too fast, assumed too much. She must distance herself from what had happened and give him space—give herself space. Her heart pumped uncomfortably, banging so hard inside her chest that she thought Stewart would hear it.

Somehow she made herself return his unreadable smile. She forced laughter into her eyes and fluttered her long eyelashes at him, deliberately teasing—letting him know that for her, too, the kiss had been a casual, sophisticated exchange. 'As you say, what's a little pleasure between friends?' She tugged at his hands which were still linked behind her back.

'Now, if you don't mind releasing me,' she said gaily, 'I can serve the pudding. You've been lucky so far—no calls—but who knows how long your luck will last?'

There was no mistaking the wave of relief that passed across his face, though it was gone in an instant. He let his hands drop to her hips and landed a kiss squarely on the tip of her nose, an unmistakable, no-nonsense, totally platonic kiss.

'What a nice, sensible woman you are, Maddy.' His voice matched hers for gaiety. 'You're absolutely right.' He tapped his mobile phone on the table beside him. 'This thing's not likely to stay silent for long.'

It was silent for a quarter of an hour, a quarter of an hour which seemed endless to Maddy, trying to make irrelevant small talk and pretend that all was well as they ate their pudding.

'How will you manage without Mrs Gumbrill?' she was asking, when the mobile sprang into life.

'Oh, get someone in from the village to do a bit of cleaning and cooking for a few hours each day. I dare say one of the staff will be able to recommend somebody.'

The mobile burred again and, murmuring an apology, he picked it up.

He announced himself and listened intently, then said sharply, 'No, don't do that, no cream or lotion. Wrap her in a blanket or something to keep her top half warm and sit her in cold water. You *must* cool down the burnt areas as fast as possible. I'll be with you shortly.' He'd already left the table and was striding across the room to the kitchen.

Maddy followed him. 'What can I do?'

'Phone for an ambulance—priority, my authority. Child with badly burned legs and bottom—this is the address.' He looked grim as he scribbled on the wall pad beside the phone. 'Then follow me down to the surgery—I've got to collect the emergency bag. I'll use the back stairs. Lock up behind me and reset the alarm.' He disappeared back through the sitting room, calling over his shoulder, 'Thanks for the meal.'

By the time Maddy had finished the call to the ambulance station and made her way down the interior staircase, Stewart was about to let himself out of the staff door at the end of the corridor. As well as his surgical case, he was carrying the bulky bag always kept topped up with equipment to give high-powered first-aid care in emergencies.

It had been used only yesterday for the disastrous bull episode, Maddy recalled as she held the door open for him. Yesterday seemed a lifetime ago.

'If you feel like talking about it, let me know what happens when you get back,' she called as he hurried across the moonlit, frosty courtyard to his car.

'I might be late.'

'It doesn't matter—give me a ring.'

He stowed the bags away. 'If you're sure?'

'Positive.'

She busied herself about the flat, clearing away the remains of their meal as she brooded over the evening which had see-sawed between delight and despair. How could she have got it so wrong about that kiss? When he'd gathered her into his arms it had seemed so right.

There had been no mistaking the message—he'd wanted her as much as she'd wanted him, emotionally, physically, passionately. His lean body had been hard and taut, his tongue urgent, yet by uttering those two words 'between friends' and smiling that taunting—or maybe cynical—smile he'd shattered the tenderness that had gone before. She squirmed at the memory.

Yet his eyes had registered not dislike or cynicism but

far subtler emotions. Had they to do with his late wife? Was he still so much in love with her that she was never far from his thoughts? Had the memory intruded into that long, satisfying kiss?

Maddy sighed, wryly acknowledging that if it had been that then it had been her own fault. She had rushed her fences. Phyllis had warned her, and she would heed that warning in future and take things very, very slowly. Let Stewart make all the running. She'd just be there for him if he wanted her.

It was a great relief to have made this positive decision. All she had to do now was to exercise patience.

Maddy settled down to watch television, but found her thoughts constantly wandering to the little burns girl and wondering what the outcome to *this* emergency would be and if it might have been averted, which automatically led on to her thinking what might be done to achieve this.

Absorbed though she was in her thoughts, with one part of her mind she was listening out for Stewart's car. She heard it arrive back just before eleven and he phoned a few minutes later.

The sound of his voice in her ear made her heart go into overdrive and, praying that his news would be good, she asked breathily, 'How did it go?'

'Little Lucy Potts has been safely admitted to the burns unit,' he said, and the relief was obvious in his voice. 'She has first- and second-degree burns, a couple of them severe. It could have been worse, but the cold-water treatment helped to contain it. Her nightie caught fire and smouldered, but her mother was able to rip it off her before it got to her waist or adhered to her skin. Poor little scrap—she was in shock, but began to improve when I got some fluids and painkillers into her.'

'Did the ambulance take long to get there?'

'About forty-five minutes—not bad—but I wish there

was somewhere nearer for emergencies or that we could do more. It's the first few minutes that are so important.'

'I've been thinking about that. I believe we should concentrate on briefing parents—and children—on what to do in an emergency. We could produce our own leaflet—' She broke off. 'Sorry, too late to talk about it now. You must get some sleep before your next call-out.'

'Alison's relieving me at midnight so if all remains quiet I shall away to my bed and sleep the sleep of the just till nine—I've a late start in the morning. But I'm intrigued about your idea. We'll discuss it tomorrow. And, Maddy...'

'Yes?'

'Thanks for this evening, it was really special. I enjoyed the meal and your company—your warmth, the conversation. It was so good to have someone to talk to who understands, who isn't bored by shop talk. I hope tonight is the beginning of...' There was a pause, then he added in a low, even voice, 'What I'm trying to say, Madeleine, and doing it badly, is that I'd value your friendship.'

Her heart seemed to thud to a halt and she found herself holding her breath. Was this a warning not to expect too much, a reminder to discount the kiss, or a subtle way of saying that the kiss had mattered and he hoped for more than friendship? Was he overcoming years of reserve or retreating behind it? Play it down, she reminded herself. Let him make the running.

Silently she let out her pent-up breath. 'And I'd value *your* friendship, too, Stewart.'

'Goes without saying. You've got it. Can't believe it's only just over a week since we met. It seems sometimes as if... Well, suffice it to say...' He groaned. 'Hell, not again. I'll have to ring off—the answerphone's blinking at me. I guess it's another call-out. See you in the morning.' His voice dropped to a throaty rumble. 'Goodnight, love.'

Love! Her heartbeat soared. 'Goodnight,' she breathed.

A week later Maddy stood at the sitting-room window with her forehead pressed against the cold glass pane, gazing down on the courtyard. She had just finished her breakfast, or what passed for breakfast—a slice of crumpled toast and half a cup of coffee—and was steeling herself to go down to the surgery. Something she'd had to do every morning for the past week.

'But not any more,' she muttered. Today she was going to put an end to it—she'd had enough.

It had been a rotten week, starting from the day after Mrs Gumbrill's departure—though that had begun well enough.

She had gone on duty in a state of gentle euphoria, well rested, having been lulled to sleep by Stewart's phone call—the half-spoken phrases and his farewell uttered in such a tender tone.

Phyllis had already been in the treatment room, turning out cupboards. With shrewd eyes she'd inspected Madeleine's face.

'Don't tell me, it was a rip-roaring success—your intimate candle-lit dinner with the boss.'

Maddy grinned. 'You could say that, but it wasn't candle-lit. I didn't have any candles in house.'

'Then you'd better stock up, my girl, ready for repeat performances.'

'Yes, I rather think I had,' Maddy murmured, a faraway expression in her eyes.

'Heaven help us,' Phyllis snorted. 'The woman's besotted. What with Alison, that makes two of you off the planet. Do you think you can come down to earth long enough to do a stocktake before work proper begins?'

'I'm right with you,' said Maddy with a laugh.

Later, when they had finished stocktaking and had time for a breather before their first patient was due, Maddy imparted the news about Mrs Gumbrill having taken herself off in high dudgeon after Stewart had spoken to her.

'Doesn't surprise me,' said Phyllis, 'but better watch your back, Maddy. She's not going to take this lying down. She'll cause trouble for you and Stewart if she possibly can.'

'There isn't much she can do, is there?' asked Maddy.

Phyllis gave her a pitying smile. 'Don't you believe it,' she said laconically. 'She'll think of something.'

It turned out to be an unusually busy day. A stomach bug of some sort had hit the village, not in epidemic proportions but affecting enough people for the doctors to send along a steady stream of patients for blood tests.

Stewart looked in late in the morning on his way to do visits.

He smiled pleasantly at the patient Maddy was treating and apologised for interrupting. 'May I have a word, Sister?' he said.

Maddy, about to take blood pressure, left the cuff in position around the patient's upper arm but didn't inflate it. 'Back in a minute,' she promised, as she followed Stewart out of the cubicle.

His eyes, pearly grey again this morning, met hers. Her heart performed its usual acrobatics.

'I've been summoned to County Hall this afternoon so we won't be able to discuss your prompt action idea,' he said. 'Mull it over with Phyllis, put something down on paper and we can talk it over at the next staff meeting.'

'OK, will do.' Greatly daring, she put a hand on his arm. 'By the way, what are you doing for lunch with no Mrs Gumbrill to cook it for you?'

'Rustle up a sandwich.'

'I could lay on soup if you want something hot.'

He looked down at her hand and then up into her eyes again.

His eyes looked different, wary. Don't push it, she reminded herself. She reddened and let her hand drop.

'Thank you, nice thought, but I think not. Don't know when I'll be back, for one thing.'

He was smiling, trying to let her down lightly, but he might as well have dashed cold water in her face.

She made her amber eyes sparkle, returned his smile and said jauntily, 'Well, you're not missing much—it would only have been out of a tin.' Turning on her heel, she whisked herself back around the cubicle curtains.

For the rest of the morning and into the afternoon Maddy tried to concentrate on work, not to mind what had happened, but her heart ached. Yesterday evening had promised so much, but it was as if his refusal to let her give him lunch—his whole manner—had pricked a bubble of hope, which had started to deflate—and her with it.

She deflated even further late in the afternoon. She went to collect a patient from the waiting room, who declared to a surprised and embarrassed audience that he wouldn't be treated by a newcomer who got loyal workers the sack. Maddy felt ready to burst into tears or sock him one—she wasn't sure which.

Her first instinct was to explain that Mrs Gumbrill hadn't been sacked, but she squashed it. This was no place to indulge in a slanging match with a cantankerous, beefy, middle-aged man, stinking of beer and tobacco, who was probably another relative of the unlamented housekeeper. So, propped up by natural and professional pride, she simply stated blandly that if he cared to wait Sister Taylor would see him and then called her next patient, who came like a lamb.

*   *   *

That had been the first day. Since then similar incidents, humiliating and hurtful, had snowballed daily so that putting in an appearance in the waiting room had become an agony.

On the plus side there *were* some patients who were happy to see her, some through indifference as to what was going on or regulars, like Mrs Jerome of the cheese counter with her varicose ulcer and Mrs Moor, battling with her weight, both of whom made a point of asking for her.

She was grateful to them and others who were supportive and quietly let her know where their sympathies lay. It was heart-warming.

But it wasn't only patients who made it plain where their sympathies lay. To Maddy's dismay, a couple of the receptionists and the cleaning ladies had cold-shouldered her in the most obvious fashion. The rest of the staff, spearheaded by Phyllis and Karen, made it abundantly clear that they were behind her but, while appreciating this, she felt guilty for splitting staff loyalties.

It was a state of affairs that couldn't go on.

Which is why she had resolved to take action, and had arranged to see the partners before morning surgery began. She hadn't even told Phyllis of her intention. It wasn't a meeting that she relished.

She pressed harder against the cold glass. All three doctors' cars were in the courtyard. She looked at her fob-watch—time to go down and face them.

CHAPTER EIGHT

'WHAT do you mean, resign?' Alison squeaked in surprise when the four of them were gathered in Stewart's office and Madeleine had delivered her bombshell.

'Just because of the departure of that old gorgon, Mrs G,' said Mike.

'Yes.'

'Why, for heaven's sake?' asked Alison. 'I know things are a bit sticky at the moment, but it's just a storm in a teacup. It'll blow itself out.'

Mike frowned. 'It's only a few of her old cronies, making trouble and scurrilous gossip. Stick it out, Maddy, the whole practice is right behind you.'

Maddy flicked a glance towards Stewart, who was sitting with his head down, resting his chin on his linked hands. Her heart thumped painfully. Was he right behind her or didn't he care that she was being ostracised by some of the patients? Had he been avoiding her? She had no means of knowing as, apart from work talk, they'd hardly exchanged a word over the last week since he'd shrugged off her offer of lunch and they'd parted in a downbeat fashion.

True, they'd been hard pressed for a few days, working to contain the bug that had started that morning, and there'd been little time for socialising, but over the last couple of days the pressure had eased off and he'd still made no attempt to talk to her, other than when on duty, and the feeling had grown that he was avoiding her.

Why didn't he say something now?

He lifted his head and focused his eyes on hers, as if to speak, but before he could do so she burst out, all the

121

frustration and hurt of the past week in her voice, 'But the whole practice isn't behind me or, what's far worse, behind Stewart. Some of the receptionists and the cleaners aren't. They believe that he sacked Mrs Gumbrill and I put him up to it.

'And because she's poisoned half the villagers against him, and painted me as a kind of whore, he can't even get domestic help in his house. That's why it makes sense if I go—better for him, better for the practice.'

Pale-faced and breathing heavily, she leaned back in her chair.

'No.' Stewart thundered out the word and thumped the table.

Madeleine and Alison jumped and Mike darted him a surprised look. 'No, you're not going anywhere.'

Madeleine experienced a surge of hope—he didn't want her to go!

He growled, 'Mike's right. It's just poisonous gossip and it *will* die a natural death. If you go you'll be giving in to it and that really would do the practice harm because you would have been driven out by a handful of bigoted bullies. Mrs G and her cronies would have a field day.'

His grey eyes collided with hers across the desk. She could read nothing in them—her own were glittering with sudden rage and disappointment. Did he care only for the practice, with no sympathy for her at all?

She put the question into words and ground out, 'Do you only care about the practice—don't you care about me? It's been hell this past week, having people saying—implying—that we... And you've not even...' And I wouldn't have minded if it had been true, she wanted to cry out.

She realised that Stewart was talking in a dry voice tinted with exasperation, as if he were explaining to a child. 'Sought you out and apologised, reassured? But, don't you see, I've *purposely* been avoiding you except when on duty so as not to add fuel to the fire? I wanted to spare you further embarrassment, make it absolutely plain that there is nothing going on between us except a working relationship.'

He shrugged broad shoulders and his lean, hard muscles tensed beneath the blue-and-white-striped sleeves of his shirt. He compressed his mobile, expressive mouth into a firm line.

Maddy stared at it, her mind going back to the evening when he had held her in his arms and kissed her... She dragged her wayward thoughts back to the present.

He was saying, 'I thought it would take the heat off you a bit. Clearly I was wrong and tongues have continued to wag. But it won't go on for ever. As for domestic help, it'll sort itself out in time. So no more nonsense about leaving—and, before you get any ideas to the contrary, I'm not saying that just to preserve the good name of the practice but because we *want* you to stay.'

Mike grinned and raised a clenched fist in mock celebration. 'I'll second that.'

Alison said quietly, 'Stewart's right. You must stay, Maddy. You're already part of the team.'

'I agree with Alison,' said Stewart. 'You fit in, not simply because you're a top-notch nurse but because we like you for yourself. We like having you around.' His voice was casual, almost nonchalant, but there was nothing casual about the way he was staring into her eyes— deeply, hypnotically.

Maddy stared back at him and read the message— surely he was almost pleading with her to stay? Her spine tingled and the hairs on the back of her neck and arms lifted and quivered. Some basic instinct told her that he was really telling her that *he* liked having her around, and that for casual and nonchalant she should read warm and sincere.

All the determination she'd mustered, before making her difficult offer to resign, oozed away as she looked at the three doctors. She was immensely touched by their support. Alison and Mike had made it quite clear that they wanted her to stay. As for Stewart, there was no doubting how he felt. It made a nonsense of her decision to go, and deep in her heart she knew that it was the last thing she wanted to do.

They were waiting for her answer.

'Well, in that case,' she said, with a smile, 'I don't see how I can refuse.'

Mike winked at her and flicked back a lock of fair hair. 'Great, you've made my day, Maddy. Nice to know that you'll still be around to bring a little sunshine into our humdrum lives.'

She used the stock answer to that. 'Flattery will get you everywhere, Dr Roach,' she said.

He grinned. 'I should be so lucky.'

Alison beamed. 'So pleased you're going to stay, Maddy. I'm sure you've made the right decision.' She looked at her watch. 'Lord, you'll have to excuse me, I must get weaving.' She stood and made for the door.

Mike also rose. 'I'll come with you,' he said, with a nod towards Stewart and Madeleine. 'I want a word about a youngster who's just come on to my list. I'm sure he's asthmatic, and I'd like you to have a look at him. Do you think...?' His voice was lost as the door closed behind them.

Silence descended on the room like a blanket. For endless moments Madeleine and Stewart sat like statues, staring at each other, their eyes locked, oblivious of everything but the unspoken vibes, flowing between them...

A distant telephone shrilled and went on and on, getting louder and louder. It stopped, and Maddy heard a voice—Stewart's voice—saying from miles away, 'Right, I'll be starting soon.'

She felt a sense of *déjà vu*. Memory stirred—same scenario, it had happened before. The spell was broken. She blinked at the grey eyes, still holding hers, inhaled a long, deep breath and let it out slowly. 'I must go,' she whispered.

'Yes.' Nothing else, just one word, sounding as if it had been dredged up from deep in his chest. He stood, crossed to the door and held it open. In a curiously detached state, Maddy drifted after him.

Stewart laid a hand on her arm as she reached him. 'We must talk some time,' he murmured, his voice still very deep. 'Get a few things straightened out. I think I may have... Oh, my dear, I wouldn't hurt you for the world.'

She smiled up at him. 'I know,' she said huskily, floating away along the corridor.

She brought herself down to earth when she reached the treatment room.

Phyllis was already dealing with an early patient in her cubicle. Maddy called out a cheerful greeting and prepared to start work on her own list of patients.

The wonderful feeling of elation stayed with her throughout the morning, though in practical terms nothing had changed. Two patients on her list asked pointedly to see Phyllis, and one of the hostile receptionists received her request for a patient's record in freezing silence. But somehow, cocooned by the doctors' generous support, knowing without reservation that they were solidly behind her, it hurt less than it had previously.

How could she ever have doubted that Stewart cared? Of course he cared. He'd made that very clear. His words, his tenderness, had filled her with joy, made her feel cherished in a way she'd not experienced before.

The word 'love' hadn't passed his lips, but she felt it was there, hovering just beneath the surface.

The word haunted her between patients, and she found herself singing softly as she binned some dirty dressings. 'Love is the sweetest thing...'

'That's an oldy—haven't heard it for donkey's years,' called Phyllis, who was tidying her cubicle. 'Surprised you know it.'

'It was a favourite of a lovely old lady I used to visit. She'd been a singer, and knew loads of old songs.'

'Ah, that accounts for it. And I must say it's nice to hear you singing. You've been so down in the dumps over this Gumbrill business I began to despair of you ever getting back to normal. Going to tell me what's brought about this metamorphosis?'

'I offered my resignation to the partners this morning and they refused to accept it.'

Phyllis said drily, 'Did you think they would?'

'I wasn't sure how they really felt about this Gumbrill business and if, by staying, I was making things worse, but they were too nice to give me my marching orders.'

'I bet they soon disabused you of that idea.'

'They did—made it plain that they wanted me to stay.'

'Of course they did.' Phyllis grinned. 'They'd have had me to contend with if they'd let you go. I really don't want to have to break in another greenhorn just as you're getting useful.'

'Thanks a bunch,' said Maddy with a laugh.

Wednesday, always a busy day, continued to live up to its reputation.

Halfway through the afternoon Mrs Penberthy, an eighty-six-year-old lady, arrived for her regular intra-muscular injection of iron. Maddy had attended her on her first day at the centre and had been amazed that, in spite of her anaemia, she was agile and chirpy. Today she arrived leaning heavily on two sticks and, though smiling, was obviously in pain.

'You've been in the wars,' said Maddy, lowering the couch to accommodate her elderly patient. 'Tell me what happened.' She helped Mrs Penberthy to turn on her side and adjust her clothes to expose one buttock ready for the injection.

'Had a fall in the garden this morning. Think I may have sprained my knee or something. It's giving me gyp.'

'You should have phoned. Someone could have called and given you your jab.'

'You're busy enough, without me taking up your time. Besides, I only live a few yards down the street—the exercise is good for me.'

'Not if you've sprained your knee, especially without support. May I have a look at it when I've finished this?' With practised fingers, Maddy firmed up a fold of the elderly, flabby flesh between thumb and forefinger, swabbed it and darted in the needle, slowly releasing the Imferon into the muscle.

Mrs Penberthy waited till the needle was withdrawn and the puncture mark sealed off with a spot plaster, before answering. 'Thank you, Sister. You did that very nicely—didn't feel a thing. Yes, if it's no bother, I'd like you to look at my knee.'

She rolled down her stocking, exposing her grossly swollen and inflamed right knee. Maddy laid gentle fingers on it. It was hot.

Mrs Penberthy winced. 'It's a bit tender,' she said.

'You don't say,' said Maddy drily. 'How on earth did you manage to walk with it in that condition?'

'With some difficulty,' said the old lady with a smile. 'Do you think it's sprained?'

'At least,' replied Maddy. 'Stay put. I want Dr Trellawney to have a look at this.'

She phoned Stewart and put him in the picture.

'I'll come at once,' he said. 'I've finished seeing patients for the afternoon, though I've so much paperwork to do, before whizzing off to Plymouth tomorrow for a conference, I reckon I'll be here till midnight.'

'Poor old you,' sympathised Maddy, a wave of pleasure washing over her. For the first time in over a week he sounded more like his usual self with her, relaxed, unguarded.

He arrived a few minutes later.

'It's more than a simple sprain. It's bursitis—inflammation of the synovial membrane surrounding the joint, producing lots of fluid,' he explained, straightening from the couch after he'd finished his examination. 'Commonly known as water on the knee.'

'Wondered if it might be that,' said Mrs Penberthy.

He smiled down at the elderly woman. 'You've done it this time, Dora, you old stoic. Now you'll have to rest. It's going to be some time before you're pottering around the garden again.'

Dora grimaced. 'So, what are you going to do about it, then, to get me back on my pins?'

'Initially, fill you with painkillers and anti-inflammatory agents,' said Stewart. He turned to Maddy. 'An intramuscular of dihydrocodeine 30mg for the pain, Sister, but I'll have to look up an anti-inflammatory that won't clash with the anaemia—'

'What, more injections?' Dora broke in.

'Afraid so—to give you an initial boost, though I'll prescribe tablets for you to take at home.'

'My poor old B.T.M.'

Stewart grinned sympathetically. 'I'm sure Sister will be very gentle,' he said, giving Maddy a warm smile and sending her heart soaring.

'Sure she will be. She's good with a needle. So, what other tortures are you going to inflict on me?'

'Apply an ice pack, fix a specially treated cooling pack around your knee and strap it into position with a support bandage, then send you home to rest. Is Sam with you?'

'No, I told him not to bother to get the car out—didn't seem worth it.'

'I'll phone him to come and collect you. You've got to keep off this leg, Dora. Keep it up, make yourself comfortable on that sofa bed of yours. You've got a downstairs loo so there's no need for you to go upstairs at all. I'll be in tomorrow to see if there's any improvement, and if the water round the joint hasn't begun to disperse I might have to draw some off.'

'Glory be! Not another needle.'

'May not be necessary if you do as you're told for once and rest.' He patted her hand. 'I'm off now. Leave you to Sister's tender mercy.' He gave another teasing smile to Maddy. 'She'll do all that's necessary. See you in the morning.'

'He'm be a right card,' said Dora in her thick Cornish accent as Stewart disappeared round the curtain, 'and a good doctor—almost as good as the old 'un.'

'Yes, so I believe,' said Maddy, delighted on Stewart's behalf with the compliment. She busied herself at the dressings trolley.

'That's why,' said Dora, 'all this nonsense that's going around is just that—nonsense.' She stared hard at Maddy with faded blue eyes. 'And don't you let it worry you, Sister. It's but a storm that'll blow itself out. There are plenty in the village who are behind you.' She paused, her eyes very knowing, and added, 'And the doctor.'

With this hopeful pronouncement going round in her head, Maddy worked her way through the remaining patients on her list. As if to endorse what Dora Penberthy had said, they were all pleasant and co-operative. Perhaps, she dared to hope, the storm *was* beginning to blow itself out.

At a quarter to five she had only one patient left to see—Janet Jerome, her cheese counter lady. Maddy was surprised. Janet wasn't due for a change of dressing on her ulcer for another couple of days—unless it had deteriorated.

'Well, it's feeling hot and itchy,' said Janet, in answer to Maddy's question when Maddy collected her from the waiting room. 'It feels as if it's oozing or something, and it aches a bit when I stand for any length of time.'

'Which is surely most of the time in your job.'

'Well, I walk about a bit backwards and forwards.' She sounded defensive. 'Look, Sister, I can't afford to give up my job. In fact—' she lowered her voice, sounding almost conspiratorial '—I was wondering…is the doctor still looking for someone to do some cleaning for him?'

'Well, he was this morning,' said Maddy, removing the soiled dressing and exposing the ulcer.

'Do you think he'd be interested if I offered to do a few hours a week?'

'I should imagine he'd be delighted, as long as he doesn't think it will harm your leg.'

'Well, I won't be standing still if I'm pushing a vacuum-cleaner around that big house of his, will I?'

'True enough,' said Maddy, 'but you can ask him yourself. I'm going to get him to have a look at this— he may want to change the treatment.'

'It's not worse, is it?' asked Janet in an alarmed voice.

'On the contrary—better! The muck's all gone, that's why it feels sticky and itchy, but the wound itself is clean. I think Dr Trellawney will prescribe a healing dressing.'

Which is precisely what he did a few minutes later.

'It's well on the mend,' he told Janet. He turned to Madeleine. 'I think a wash-out with normal saline, don't you, Sister, then a collodion dressing to dry and form a protective seal?'

'Yes, and a padded support bandage from ankle to knee...' Spoken breathily, the prosaic suggestion somehow came out sounding incredibly sexy. Madeleine blushed.

Stewart's eyes flared for an instant with...amusement? Appreciation? He nodded. 'Please—do that.'

He smiled down at Janet, propped up on the couch. 'I thought at one time we might have to do a skin graft, but it doesn't look as if there's going to be any need for that now because you've stuck to your treatment and it's paid off—well done.' He patted her shoulder. 'I've got to be off now. See Sister next week—she'll check it out. Any more problems, let me know.'

'Thank you, Doctor, and...' She hesitated and looked at Maddy.

'Go on, ask the doctor, he won't bite,' said Maddy encouragingly.

'I'm intrigued,' said Stewart. 'Ask away.'

'Sister said that you're still looking for a cleaner for The Old House, Doctor.'

'I am. Why, do you know someone who might help me out?'

'Yes—me. I could do just a few hours a week—some mornings, just cleaning, not cooking.'

He frowned. 'Are you sure, Janet? Haven't you got enough on your plate with the shop, the kids, Eddy?'

'I need the money, Doctor,' Janet replied simply. 'And I'd like to work for you. You've been kindness itself over the last few years, helping me sort things out when Eddy was in prison. It makes me that mad that you can't get someone to do a bit of housework for you just because of the rumours old Grace Gumbrill's set about.'

Stewart said grimly, 'You know it won't be easy for you if you come to work at The Old House. Eddy's family being remotely related to the Gumbrill's, they'll accuse you of going over to the enemy.'

'So what's new? I'm not scared of *her*. Grace's never had a good word to say for me—and when was things ever easy for me, Doctor? I can take anything that lot can dish out…unless…' She stared hard at him, and then said slowly, 'Unless, of course, it would make it awkward for you, employing the wife of a gaolbird—I wouldn't want to do that. Or perhaps you think he might nick something from you, but, I promise I won't let him near the house.'

Stewart looked astonished. 'Good Lord, the thought hadn't even crossed my mind. If you're game, I certainly am. The house is a tip at the moment.' His mouth curled into a sardonic smile. 'You might say it's lacking a woman's touch.' He pulled back the cubicle curtain. 'Come to my room as soon as Sister has finished dealing with your leg, and we'll get things sorted out so that you can come to my rescue as soon as possible.'

'Would tomorrow be too soon, Doctor?'

'Brilliant,' he said, as he disappeared around the curtain.

The phone rang just as Maddy finished eating supper and she knew it was Stewart before she picked up the receiver. Her hand shook slightly.

'Hello,' she murmured, cursing the give-away huskiness when she had meant to sound calm and controlled. Cool it, she reminded herself.

'You sound as if you've got laryngitis,' he said with a chuckle.

'Well, if I have, you don't sound very sympathetic,' she snapped. She tried to clear her throat.

'Sorry, I would be if you had it—I'd be over like a shot, dosing you up with all kinds of medication and tons of sympathy.'

Maddy almost dropped the receiver. She could imagine his wide, mobile mouth, curving into a smile. Was this the reserved Stewart Trellawney, talking—no, *flirting* like Mike Roach? She wasn't quite sure how to handle it—flirt back? 'Flirt'—an old-fashioned word that seemed to fit. It was nothing like the head-on brashness of the modern approach, but gentle, teasing. She liked it.

'That would be nice,' she purred. 'Pity I'm not lying pale, wan and feverish on my sickbed.'

'If you were pyrexic you'd have a hectic flush and be sweating buckets.'

'How very romantic!' She tried to sound sarcastic but spoilt the effect by giggling. She felt gloriously light-hearted.

'Medically speaking, it's the plain, unvarnished truth... But I didn't phone to discuss your mythical illness, however fascinating, but to confirm that Janet is starting work tomorrow. I thought you'd like to know as you were concerned about how I was managing. It'll be a treat, having her around. She's such a nice woman and deserves a break after all she's been through.'

It was a sobering thought. 'What was her husband in prison for?'

'Burglary—he's a repeat offender. He's been out a few weeks and can't get a job—that's why she's so hard up. And with two teenagers to support...'

'Poor Janet,' said Maddy softly, and then added fiercely, 'I'm so glad you've given her the job, Stewart. But will it make things even more difficult for you, employing her, because her husband's been in prison?'

'Not at all. Might add a few small-minded folk to Grace Gumbrill's hate-Dr-Trellawney brigade.' Maddy could picture him, shrugging his broad shoulders. 'But that doesn't matter. Believe me, it'll be to our mutual benefit, Janet's and mine.'

'Pity she can't do any cooking. You'll still have to forage for yourself.'

'*You* have to forage for yourself.'

'But my hours are more predictable than yours.'

'A tin of beans takes all of five minutes to cook—very nourishing, beans on toast.'

'But can get monotonous. And no vegetables—most unhealthy.'

'Are you offering to supplement my baked-bean diet with a more balanced one, Sister Coleman?'

They were teasing each other, gently, intimately, in the manner of old and loving friends. It was deeply satisfying.

'Just the occasional casserole, nothing exotic.'

'Talking of exotic…do you like Italian, foodwise?'

'Love it, all that pasta and fresh vegetables.'

'There's a new place opened in St Ives called The Italian Place—it's already getting quite a reputation. I'd like to take you there for a meal, build up some credit for all those healthy dishes you're going to feed me with. Will you be free some time over the weekend?'

'I'm having lunch with Phyllis and her mother on Sunday, but I'm not doing anything on Saturday, apart from going into Penruth to shop.'

Suddenly he was serious, no longer teasing but asking formally, 'So will you have dinner with me on Saturday, Madeleine?'

Her heart turned over. She was suffused by a tide of almost maternal affection as it dawned on her that this usually reserved and self-assured man was out of practice, dating a woman.

'Well, will you?' he said.

Squashing down a desire to yell, yes, yes, yes, she replied sedately, 'I'd like that.'

'I'll pick you up at seven… Goodnight, Madeleine.'

'Goodnight.'

She decided to phone Fee and Naomi, before going to bed, to update them on what had happened. They would be at Naomi's. When she had last phoned she had been desperately miserable and unable to conceal it, and they had been lovingly sympathetic and concerned. She owed them the good news.

'Oh, Maddy, that's great,' said Fee, when she'd finished giving them an edited account of the day. 'We thought last week that you were going to turn up on the doorstep, begging for shelter.'

'I almost did—would have done if the medics hadn't backed me up.'

'Don't you mean one medic in particular?' asked Naomi slyly.

'No, I mean all of them.'

'But I thought you were nuts about the dishy Dr Trellawney.'

'I am…that is… Look, I had to know that they all wanted me to stay. We're a group practice and it's important that we show a united front to the village. But Stewart's support *is* especially important to me—in fact, I wouldn't stay without it. By the way, he's taking me out to dinner on Saturday—satisfied?'

'Alleluia, that's much more like it,' enthused Naomi.

'Glad to hear he's taking you out,' said Fee. 'You deserve a treat after the angst you've been through. Make the most of it, and take care, old thing, we worry about you. Remember there's always a bed for you here if you need it.'

'That won't be necessary now, but thanks.'

They talked for a few more minutes, exchanging gossip about mutual friends, and then rang off.

Madeleine went to bed and slept soundly until morning. It was the best night's sleep she'd had for over a week. She woke, feeling on top of the world.

Even the fact that she would see hardly anything of Stewart over the next couple of days, because of the conference in Plymouth, failed to dent her euphoria. She hated the thought that he wouldn't be around, but savoured the thought that they would be meeting on Saturday on more intimate terms away from the health centre.

He called in at the treatment room to say goodbye as she and Phyllis were preparing for afternoon surgery.

'Look after the shop while I'm away, ladies. I'll not be back till late on Friday.' He smiled at them both, but his gaze lingered for a moment longer on Madeleine.

She missed him from the moment he walked out of the door, but it made the prospect of seeing him on Saturday more exciting—like waiting to open presents on Christmas Day.

Over the past week, unnoticed in her unhappiness, winter seemed to have become spring. The short days were warmed by the pale sun. Sturdy plants began to push through the rich, brown earth that filled the tubs dotted round the courtyard.

It's exactly how I feel, thought Maddy as she took a breath of fresh air during her lunch-break on Friday, lightly touching the spears of green emerging from snow-bound hibernation—as if I'm emerging out of the cold darkness into the light and warmth of being wanted, cherished, perhaps even...loved!

She was uplifted, enchanted, and the weather matched her frothy, ebullient mood.

'It feels like April in London without the pollution,'

she told Phyllis, to explain her bubbling happiness. 'The air's so soft, so clear, scented like wine.'

Phyllis grinned. She wasn't deceived, but she played along. 'We're not called the Cornish Riviera for nothing,' she said. 'Spring comes early to this part of the world, though we do have to watch out for an occasional late snap of frost.'

Madeleine felt a faint trickle of apprehension run up her spine.

'That,' she said, 'sounds almost like a warning.'

Phyllis surveyed her with kind humorous eyes. 'Let's say more of a gardener's hint to be prepared for whatever the weather throws at you. The thaw's set in, but winter's not yet over.'

Then, abruptly abandoning the analogy, she said, 'What I'm saying is just take care, Maddy. Gumbrill and her cronies are still out there, gunning for you and Stewart, so be on the alert, take things slowly, don't give them any ammunition.'

Madeleine pulled a face. 'They seem to be able to manufacture that for themselves,' she said, 'and living like a nun hasn't done much for me so far, has it?'

Phyllis shook her head. 'Point taken. I'm simply concerned for you both.'

'I know,' said Madeleine. 'And I know it's mad, but I can't help feeling that whatever happens everything's going to come right in the end.'

'You mean love will conquer all,' said Phyllis drily.

Madeleine threw back her head and gave a great peal of laughter. 'Something like that,' she said. 'Oh, Phyll, I feel on top of the world.'

CHAPTER NINE

MADELEINE was still feeling on top of the world when she woke on Saturday morning. Shrugging on her dressing-gown, she sped through to the sitting room, swept back the curtains and peered down into the courtyard. Stewart's car, sturdy and reassuring, was there where it should be, parked outside The Old House.

He was home, safe and sound, and she would be seeing him in a few hours' time. In just a few more hours, she thought as she went through to the kitchen. Not that I have to wait till this evening, she mused as she measured coffee into the percolator. I could ring him and invite him over for breakfast right now.

She eyed the wall phone. He could be here in minutes—her stomach churned at the thought.

She snorted in disgust. 'Cool it,' she reminded herself yet again. 'He said seven this evening so take yourself off on that wild shopping spree and keep a low profile till then.'

The church clock struck seven as Stewart rang the doorbell.

With a heart that threatened to leap from her breast Madeleine had watched him cross the lamplit courtyard, and counted to ten, before opening the door.

He stood on the platform at the top of the staircase. Madeleine stared at him, mesmerised. He looked impeccable, distinguished in a dark suit, pristine white shirt and a muted but colourful tie. His dark hair gleamed in

138

the lamplight. Surely he'd been away more than two days—it seemed like a lifetime.

'Hello,' she said breathlessly at last. She knew she should move, but her feet remained as if glued to the floor.

Stewart smiled, his deep-set, amused eyes crinkling at the corners as he held aloft the small gold-topped bottle he was carrying. 'Aren't you going to ask me in before this warms up? Just a two-glass size, enough to put us in the party mood. It's been chilling in the fridge all day.'

Feasting her eyes on him, it took a moment for the words to penetrate.

She blinked. 'What? Oh, yes, of course, lovely, champagne. Please, *do* come in, I'll fetch glasses.'

She unglued her feet and moved aside.

He bent his head and brushed his lips across one flushed cheek as he passed. 'It's nice to be back,' he said softly.

'Nice to have you back,' she murmured.

Nice!

Nice had nothing to do with the way she felt about this man who was standing in her kitchen, smiling his wide, tender smile and calmly surveying her with smoky-grey eyes. Was that how he felt about her—that she was milk and water nice, nothing more—or did *his* heart, like hers, perform all manner of gymnastics when he saw her?

She hoped it did. Her breathing quickened, and again she seemed rooted to the spot.

Stewart put the bottle on the worktop. 'Glasses,' he reminded her gently, 'and a bottle opener wouldn't come amiss.'

She dredged up a voice and a tremulous smile from somewhere. 'Of course. Opener's in that drawer and the glasses are here.' She spun round, opened a cupboard above her head and reached up to the top shelf.

'Here, let me.' He stood behind her and reached over her shoulder. His arm stretched up over hers, his body, hard, taut and radiating heat, moulded itself against her back. His breath fanned the top of her head, stirring her hair, and his familiar woody scent filled her nostrils. 'These?'

Madeleine nodded, holding herself rigid to stop her knees buckling. She felt like a rag doll. 'Nearest I've got to champagne glasses,' she breathed.

'They'll do. It's the vintage that goes into them that matters.' He went on nuzzling the top of her head, breathing in deeply. 'And, talking of vintage, you smell gorgeous and look ravishing—a flapper, nineteen-twenties vintage.'

He put the glasses beside the bottle, took hold of her shoulders and twirled her to face him. She could scarcely breathe. She looked up into the shining grey depths of his eyes. Her fast-beating heart fluttered against her ribcage, and her lips parted hungrily as she waited for him to take her in his arms and crush her against him, squashing her roused breasts against his hard chest.

But his arms didn't go round her. Instead, he cupped her chin in his hands and stared down at her. 'Those lovely tiger eyes,' he whispered, lowering his head till their mouths were touching. His lips melted against hers, butterfly soft, neither passionate nor demanding but affectionate and brief. He raised his head. 'I've missed you, Maddy,' he said, his thumbs feathering a circle round her eyes.

Completely poleaxed and trying desperately not to mind about the flat, nothing kind of kiss, she said shakily, 'I've missed you, too.'

'I know,' he murmured, 'but you mustn't. I've too much emotional baggage.' He frowned, and his eyes darkened. He dropped his hands from her face, picked up the bottle of champagne in one hand and the corkscrew in the other and in a voice suddenly brittle and detached said, 'A spot of this is called for, I think, to get the evening off to a good start.'

She was speechless! He had to be joking! A good start, after what had just happened? A kiss that wasn't a kiss but a veiled warning? Madeleine swallowed a great lump of bitterness that had lodged in her throat. Her heart sank like a stone. She found herself staring at his lean, competent fingers, manipulating the corkscrew. Her thoughts seemed to be corkscrewing in much the same way.

She dragged her eyes away from his hands to his profile as he concentrated on the bottle.

Through clenched teeth she said, 'I can't believe that I'm hearing this. What do you mean—*I mustn't* and *too much emotional baggage*? And what the hell was that *non*-kiss all about? Before you went away I thought...' In an effort to suppress the rage that was threatening to overwhelm her she took a deep breath and continued in a tightly controlled voice.

'What's wrong, Stewart—isn't it time you came clean with me? There's been this on-off thing between us since day one.' Her voice softened a fraction. 'Look, I know there's something bugging you, something from your past, some hurt, so tell me...' To her fury, tears pricked the back of her eyes. She gulped, sniffed and fumbled uselessly for a tissue.

Stewart thrust a large snowy-white handkerchief into her hand and said in an expressionless voice, 'You're dead right, Maddy, you deserve an explanation.'

Dully, through a blur of held-back tears, she watched him pour two glasses of wine. 'This is going to take some time. May we...?' He gestured towards the sitting room.

She blew her nose, nodded and marched, stiff-backed, out of the kitchen. 'Please, sit down.' Her voice was formal, as to a stranger. She sat in one armchair and indicated the other.

He handed her a glass and automatically she took it from him, then looked at it with distaste. 'I don't want *this*,' she said sharply. 'There's nothing to celebrate—take it away.'

'Drink it, it's medicinal.' His voice was flat, impersonal. He took a sip from his own glass and stared at her over the rim for a moment in silence.

She stared back, trying not to notice the haunted look that was back in his eyes, and said, 'Well, are you going to explain?'

'Yes, I'm just marshalling my thoughts. I want to be honest with you, Maddy, but I don't find it easy. I'm not used to baring my soul—I tend to keep my own counsel.' He ran his hands through his hair, leaving it uncharacteristically ruffled.

'So I've noticed.' Her voice was dry and hard, but she wanted to reach out and tear down Stewart's self-imposed barrier of silence. She couldn't bear to see this usually strong, confident man, whom she loved, looking so lost. She had to give him a lead, help him open up. She said quietly, 'Has it to do with your wife, dying of cancer?'

He nodded. In a voice that was harsh, cold and full of suppressed anger, he said, '*Untreated* cervical cancer, the insidious, painless disease…until it spreads to the surrounding organs. Hers did. Classic case.'

Madeleine was shocked to the core. She forgot her own anger. She stared at him in disbelief. '*Untreated*! But why? Surely she had regular smear tests—they would have shown that something was wrong early on and she could have received treatment.'

'*Smear* tests.' His voice was unbelievably bitter. 'Oh,

she had smears done, but when one showed up irregu-larities…she didn't follow it up and she didn't tell me until it was too late. And do you know *why* she didn't tell me?' His fine, intelligent eyes were glazed with pain as he stared across at Madeleine.

She shook her head. The intensity of his pain seared through her. 'Why?' she asked faintly, trying to imagine what could possibly have stopped this woman, whom he so obviously adored, from confiding in him.

'Because, God help me, I was too busy holding a shaky, overworked practice together—that was my pri-ority. I was always so tired and my patients had to come first… She didn't want to bother me. *Bother me*! Her words, not mine. So, what do you think of that, Maddy?' His voice was full of self-loathing.

'I had a good marriage with a lovely, gentle woman, and I shot it to bits. So, what do you think of a man who can let that happen? Hell, she didn't blame me even when she was dying, though it was my negligence that murdered her.'

Like a coiled spring, Madeleine leaned forward in her chair. 'Rubbish!' she spat out. 'Don't say that. She was a grown woman who made her own choice—an extraor-dinary choice, but hers. It wasn't your fault that she didn't tell you.'

'But it was. If I had not taken my marriage for granted, given my wife some of the attention that I gave to my patients, I'd have noticed that she was worried about something—that our sex life was practically non-existent. But it was months before I realised that she was losing weight and having erratic periods, by which time the tumour had spread and invaded the pelvic organs and she was beginning to get pain.'

'But even then…surely, surgery, radiotherapy, laser treatment?'

'Radical surgery was the only option, and that meant

removal of *all* the damaged organs. It might have given her a few more months, years perhaps, but Thea turned it down flat. Poor, dear love, she even joked that she wanted to take all her bits and pieces with her.' His face contorted with distress.

'It was hell, watching her die, though her pain was well controlled. She was so brave. I nursed her at home as long as I could, but eventually she had to go into the local hospice. Super place, they were so caring.' His face looked drawn and haggard. He lifted his glass to his lips and seemed surprised to find it empty.

Madeleine resisted the desire to wrap her arms around him and give him a hug, not a sexy one but a loving and reassuring one. She removed the empty glass from his stiff fingers, and said matter-of-factly, 'You need a whisky and then coffee, and so do I.'

'Thank you.' He looked through and beyond her.

He was still staring into space when she returned from the kitchen a few minutes later. She put a glass into his hand. 'Whisky and water,' she said, as she returned to her own armchair.

'Thanks.' He frowned and refocused, seeming to see her for the first time. He cleared his throat and said in a stony voice, 'I apologise. I shouldn't be subjecting you to all this. I'm being maudlin.'

'No, you're not. You're talking, which is what you should have done ages ago,' Madeleine said quietly. 'There's a limit to keeping a stiff upper lip, and I think you've about reached yours. So, go on talking, Stewart. Don't clam up on me—let me help just by listening. I realise that…'

Stewart's grave grey eyes searched her face. 'What do you realise, Maddy?'

She gulped down a mouthful of whisky. 'That you don't want a close relationship with me—at least not yet. You haven't got over your wife's death.'

'I'll *never* get over my wife's death, or the manner of it,' he said evenly. 'I thought I could when I chucked the Glasgow practice and moved down here. Thought that moving from north to south, from an inner city practice to a rural one, would help me to forget.'

'And did it?'

'Simply running away didn't help, but meeting old Dr Marric, who was a wise and compassionate man, did. He showed me how to face Thea's death and accept it but not be submerged by it. And working with a nice bunch of people, having time to be involved with my patients, helped me come to terms with it and enjoy life again in a low-key fashion. Until recently it worked—I was contented, even happy, with the way things were. I didn't feel the need for anything more.'

He'd been staring at his glass, but suddenly he looked up. The expression in his eyes made the hairs at the back of her neck quiver.

'So, what happened?' she whispered.

'*You* happened, Maddy!' His voice was deep and throaty. 'You walked into my life and turned it upside down. For the first time in years I started to come alive, to believe that it was possible to love again, but...'

'But...' she gripped her glass till her knuckles turned white. 'But something else happened, didn't it, when you were about to kiss me?'

'Yes. I looked down into your dear, lovely face and suddenly realised that I had to stop what was happening between us before it went any further. I came to my senses—knew that I couldn't be that selfish a second time around.'

Madeleine's heart was hammering out a tattoo against her chest wall, and her mouth was dry. *He loved her—* he'd as good as said it. Nothing in the world mattered except that. Her pulses raced, and the blood bounded furiously through her veins, drumming in her ears.

Calm down, she warned herself, he has reservations. What does he mean—being selfish? How can loving me be selfish when he knows that I love him, and, heaven knows, I've made that plain enough? It's as if he's trying to protect me—or is he just shying away from commitment of any kind, even friendship? A powerful hand seemed to squeeze her heart... Surely it wasn't that, it couldn't be.

She met his steady gaze across the small space that divided the two armchairs and said in a dry little voice, 'You must explain, Stewart. I don't understand what you mean by being selfish.'

'If I allow this...this attraction between us to develop you run the risk of being saddled with a man with not only a load of guilt but a man for whom, in spite of everything, work still means dedication. I'm a workaholic, Maddy, and I don't know if, with the best will in the world, I can break that addiction. It's in my genes.'

A faint, brief smile quirked at the corners of his mouth. 'Both my parents are dedicated doctors, working in Africa—the work ethic comes naturally to me.'

'And I'm a dedicated nurse, and no slouch when it comes to work.'

'I've known that since day one. You were bursting with enthusiasm, full of intelligent questions. And you've proved what a caring nurse you are every day since.'

'So I know about dedication. Why shouldn't I take this *risk*, as you call it? If I don't mind taking you on, baggage and all, why should *you*? Or are you going to reject my love to prevent your conscience pricking you? Or is it quite simply a matter of not wanting to make a commitment?'

Stewart inhaled sharply. 'My dear Maddy, you don't think that, do you?' he asked in an horrified voice. 'That I care more about keeping my conscience clear than I do about you? As for commitment, I don't want *you* to make a commitment that you might later regret. That I couldn't bear.'

Maddy stared at him in silence for a long time, and he stared back. The atmosphere crackled with unspoken questions and answers. The rich aroma of percolating coffee drifted in from the kitchen. The church clock chimed eight.

'I don't know what to think,' she said at last. 'Or what to do.' She swallowed the trickle of whisky that was left in her glass. 'I'm muddled as hell. Any suggestions, Dr Trellawney?' she asked, trying forlornly to lighten the moment.

Stewart stood abruptly, his six feet something towering over her, rock-like and authoritative. 'As a matter of fact, I have. Come on, up you get.' He took her glass from her hand, put it on the side table and pulled her to her feet. 'I suggest that you go and pour out two mugs of coffee, black and sweet, while I phone the restaurant, plead an emergency and apologise for not turning up for dinner.'

'Oh, Lord, I'd forgotten dinner—what time was our table booked for?'

'Eight. We should be miles away in St Ives right now.'

'We've talked for an hour.'

'We've had a lot to talk about, and we've not finished yet.' He squeezed her hands. 'But it'll all come right, given time and loads of patience. Perhaps that's what we need more than anything—time. I thought time didn't matter when you walked in and bowled me over, but I was wrong. We need time to get to know each other. Build a foundation of friendship. We must be sure, Maddy, sure about us.'

From out of the depths, he produced a quirky, lopsided smile. 'For two mature adults, who ought to know better, we have rather rushed our fences, haven't we?'

'It's all those pheromones,' she said, managing a laugh of sorts, relieved that his mood had lifted a little.

How gaunt he looks, she thought, examining his face with loving eyes. Not that it's surprising—the evening's been pretty traumatic. It must have hurt him to spill out all that about his wife. I wish he'd let me—

She squashed the wish, stretched up and gently kissed his cheek. 'You make your phone call and I'll go and rustle up something to eat,' she said, 'since we've missed out on dinner.'

It was good to be in the kitchen, doing things with her hands. She opened tins and heated soup, scrambled eggs and made toast like an automaton. Her mind felt empty, drained by her warring emotions. Yet in a strange way she felt at peace. They'd forge a foundation of friendship, Stewart had said.

It was a calming, comforting thought—they would build a strong, loving, fulfilled relationship. Somehow, for the time being, she would bury her urgent physical need of him and settle for that.

They ate in companionable silence, both deep in thought, trawling through all that had been said in the past hour. But over coffee they talked about all manner of things—books, television, the state of the world, the health service, anything that had touched their lives—and found, to their intense satisfaction, that they had much in common.

It was a further bonding, a beginning. They had started the process of getting to know each other.

By mutual consent, though, they avoided exchanging any more emotional intimacies, silently agreeing that they had enough to digest for the present. More would be like eating too much rich food.

When they were parting for the night Stewart cupped

Madeleine's face in his hands and said softly, 'We've talked of me tonight, Maddy, but next time I want to hear all about you—about your family, where you grew up, what your ambitions were as a small girl. In fact, I want to know all there is to know about you.' His eyes were infinitely warm and tender.

'Is that all?' she replied with a laugh, suppressing a faint twinge of apprehension. What would he make of her chequered early history as a child in foster care? 'Aren't I allowed to keep any secrets?'

'Not from me, you're not,' he said firmly. 'Grim as it is, I've come clean about mine. It's only fair that you should do the same.' He smiled. 'Anyway, my love, I can't imagine you having any big, bad secrets to hide.'

'Wanna bet?' she said lightly.

He stared down into her eyes and seemed to read something there. 'If you have, Maddy, please share them with me.' His voice was deadly serious. He brushed a kiss across both her cheeks. 'Till next time,' he murmured, before plunging down the lamplit staircase. He paused at the bottom to turn and raise his hand in a farewell salute.

CHAPTER TEN

As it turned out, the next time was not as soon as either of them would have wished. Despite Stewart being constantly in Madeleine's mind, it seemed that the fates were hell-bent on keeping them apart.

Pressure of work and dealing with an outbreak of sore throats added to the usual volume of patients with coughs, colds and other winter ills, increasing everyone's workload over the next few days. Madeleine was kept busy, taking, labelling and despatching swabs for analysis and increasing her normal treatment lists so that sometimes they drifted over into the evenings.

As for Stewart, he was working all hours, starting early and finishing late, either in surgery or out on calls. He was covering not only his own patients but, in addition, covering for Mike who was on leave. The locum who had been booked in had fallen foul of the ski slopes and had ended up with two broken legs, and no suitable substitute was available at short notice. Alison had taken on some of the work, but she had to cope with two large asthma clinics, which couldn't be postponed, so the bulk of the work fell to Stewart.

Madeleine saw him return late one evening and let himself into his dark, empty house, and felt an aching desire to do something practical to make life easier for him. After all, they were supposed to be laying the foundations of friendship. Perhaps occasionally she would feed him, invite him for a meal—at least she could make sure that he had something hot to return home to.

But she wouldn't invite him—she would take something to him. That way he could keep it hot should he be called out before he finished eating. Besides, taking it to him would seem more of a practical arrangement than a social event.

It was just after nine o'clock the following evening when she saw him pull up and park in his usual place. He climbed the steps slowly and let himself into the house. Her heart contracted—he looked dead beat.

She gave him a few minutes and then, armed with a laden tray, she crossed the courtyard and knocked on the front door.

Stewart opened it almost at once. He was holding a pile of envelopes which he was obviously sorting through. He stared at her in surprise. 'Good Lord, what on earth are you doing here?'

Her heart sank. As a greeting it didn't rate much. It hadn't occurred to her that he might not be pleased to see her.

She nodded toward the tray. 'I know you haven't had time to eat,' she said, 'so I thought that supper wouldn't come amiss. But I won't come in, I'll leave it. I can see that you're dog-tired.'

A wide smile lit up his face, wiping out the tired lines. 'Oh, Maddy, of course you must come in.' He took her arm and almost dragged her into the hall. 'Apologies for the less than enthusiastic welcome. I thought for a moment you were another patient and I was girding my loins, as it were. Oh, my dear, it's so good to see you.'

Madeleine laughed as relief flooded over her. 'You saw me this afternoon,' she reminded him.

'Messing around with swabs and specimen bottles, surrounded by patients—I don't count that.'

He looked down at her. The fierce, hungry expression

in his eyes made her pulses gallop. Her spine prickled and her arms trembled, making the tray rattle gently.

'Here, I'll take that.' His voice was gruff, abrupt. He relieved her of the tray and inhaled theatrically. 'This smells good—manna to a starving man.' He turned away and said brusquely, 'Follow me. We'll eat in the kitchen.'

She didn't mind his brusqueness. He wants me as much as I want him, she thought exultantly as she followed him along the corridor, but he doesn't want to admit it. He's determined on keeping up this friendship-only thing.

At first sight the kitchen looked cosy and old-fashioned, with its square pine table and Windsor arm-chairs, but carefully blended in were a modern, gleaming Aga, a microwave, a dishwasher and a range of fitted wall cupboards.

Madeleine stopped in the doorway. It's a family kitchen, she thought, and it should be full of children, dogs, cats, cooking smells—not just a single man. She quietly drew in her breath…

Stewart set the tray on the table. 'Impressed?'

She pushed aside hopeful, sentimental thoughts of a houseful of children and animals. 'Very. I expected it to be dark and full of Victoriana like the parlour.'

'It was when I inherited it, but I fought and won the battle with Mrs G to have it modernised. Though she would never admit it, she loved and guarded it with her life. I was hardly allowed over the threshold—now I practically live in it.'

'I'm not surprised. The kitchen's the heart of a house.'

He smiled into her eyes and said softly. 'Talking of heart, I poured mine out to you the other night, Maddy. Now it's your turn.'

She smiled back and nodded. Over the last few days

she'd had time to think about it and knew that she owed him the plain, unvarnished truth. She had to let him see that she had emotional baggage, too, and would need his understanding and support. 'Fair enough,' she said, 'but not yet. We both need to eat—let's have supper first.'

Over supper they talked of taking on another doctor. The practice needed a fourth doctor, or at least a part-timer, now that it had expanded to cover more outlying villages—a learner GP, perhaps, someone whom they might train to stay on permanently.

'Sounds a good idea to me,' said Madeleine. 'Anything to stop you running yourself ragged. What do Alison and Mike think?'

'They're all for it.'

'But you have reservations?'

He pulled a face. 'I'm a bit wary, it's such a big step. Maybe we should make do with a locum until we decide on what sort of help we want. It's not the best solution. The patients like—need—continuity. But rather that than take on someone who doesn't fit in.'

'Then give yourself plenty of time to find the right person, part or full time—advertise for both. Maybe two quality part-timers is the answer. That would give more flexibility, cover the sort of emergency we've got now. Whatever, I think you should get cracking soon. It's an employer's market, you'll be spoilt for choice. Go for it.'

He gave her a sharp, penetrating look. 'You're that sure?'

'Yes.'

'Right—that clinches it. I'll get on to it tomorrow. Thanks, Maddy, you're brilliant.' He stood up. 'Ready for coffee?'

Madeleine nodded. 'Please.'

A warm wave of pride washed over her as she

watched him cross to the Aga and pour the fragrant liquid from a bubbling pot. He'd asked her opinion, trusted her judgement and was prepared to act upon it. It was like another declaration of love, she thought as he returned to the table and set a mug in front of her.

He smiled down at her with great tenderness. 'Now,' he said softly, 'enough shop talk. We'll talk about you, Maddy.' He returned to his chair at the other side of the table.

Madeleine wrapped her hands round the mug and stared down at the coffee. Now that the moment had come she didn't know where to start. Stewart sat very still, waiting, and she could feel his eyes on her.

After a short silence she said tersely, 'I've been fostered or in care since I was four. I don't remember my father and have only the vaguest memory of my mother. She cried a lot. I was found abandoned in a shopping centre in Canterbury. I knew my name and age, and the powers that be eventually traced my birthplace to Brighton, but I have never been able to trace either of my parents…and, surprise, surprise, they have never tried to track me down.'

She couldn't keep the hurt and bitterness out of her voice. It must be saying it out aloud for the first time in years, she thought, compressing her lips into a tight line. The last thing she wanted was to sound sorry for herself and tout for sympathy. She squared her shoulders and sat up very straight.

Stewart muttered an expletive. 'Oh, Maddy, I'm so sorry. So you're quite on your own. You've no family?' He got up and dragged a chair around the table and sat beside her. He didn't attempt to touch her but the close warmth of his body was comforting.

She said brightly, 'Don't make me sound like little

Orphan Annie. I'm not quite on my own. I've got Fee and Naomi and their partners—they're like family.'

'Your mates from Kits…'

'That's right, and, until a few years ago when she died, Rose—Rose Darling, the last in a long line of foster mums. She was everything that her name implied. God knows what would have happened to me if it hadn't been for her.'

'You had several foster parents?'

'Went through them like a dose of salts. I wasn't a nice child, Stewart… I was rude to people who tried to help me, lied, stole things, ran away, had a beastly temper.'

'Not surprising. You were abandoned at four, Maddy. What else were you to do to a world that had done that to you?' His voice was very gentle.

Maddy slid him a sideways look of surprise. 'You really understand, don't you?' she said. 'Nobody did, you know, not till I was sent to Rose when I was ten. She was patient, but not endlessly so. She wasn't afraid to lose her temper with me on occasions, just as a real mother might. We had a sort of bargain—she'd do right by me if I did right by her. It made sense.

'She and her husband ran a small farm in Kent. Should have had loads of kids but couldn't so they fostered. Bob was much older than Rose and died soon after I arrived. Perhaps that's why it worked for Rose and me…'

'You needed each other.'

'Precisely. For the first time in my life I had someone to myself… It was a wonderful feeling. She was mother, father, sisters and brothers rolled into one. I was devastated when she died.'

'What did she die of?'

'Directly a chest infection, but indirectly multiple

sclerosis. It was diagnosed when I was fourteen, though she went on working on the farm even after she was wheelchair-bound. Amazing what she still managed to do… That's when I decided to take up nursing.'

She drank the last of her coffee. 'There's just one more thing,' she said bluntly. 'If you don't want to continue with this relationship because of what I've told you, please say so now.'

He looked at her as if she were mad. 'Why the hell should I want to do that?'

'Because you might have second thoughts about making a commitment to a woman with no known family and possibly a dodgy background.'

He stared at her in silence for a moment, then said in an icy voice that sent a shiver down her spine, 'Do you really think I'm capable of behaving like that, Madeleine? Using that as an excuse not to make a commitment?' His eyes were like hard grey chips.

Her eyes slid away from his. 'No,' she said miserably, '*you* might not, but I had to ask. You see…'

'There was someone in the past who did?' His perceptiveness was breathtaking.

She nodded. 'I'd just finished my training. He was on the first rung of the surgical ladder, ambitious, and decided that the last thing he wanted was a wife without acceptable antecedents. He dumped me directly I told him.'

Her mouth quivered in an apology for a smile. 'I vowed then that *if* I ever entered into any sort of ongoing relationship I would keep quiet about my past.' She shook her head. 'But I couldn't do that to you, Stewart, after you'd been so frank with me. I had to be honest with you, whatever the outcome.'

There was a long silence. Madeleine watched his face, praying that he would understand. She saw the ice melt

from his eyes, leaving them a soft, smoky, bluish-grey.
Slowly he stood up and then, offering her his out-
stretched hands, pulled her to her feet.

Holding her at arm's length, he said gruffly, 'That
must have taken some courage. Thank you, Maddy, I
appreciate the vote of confidence. I'm amazed you can
trust me or anyone after the treatment that creep meted
out to you.' He drew her to him and wrapped his arms
around her.

His hands cupped her small, firm buttocks, moulding
her to him, then slid up over her slim hips and slender
ribcage and came to rest against the soft swell of her
breasts. 'And this,' he murmured, lowering his head, 'is
long overdue. It's to make up for the non-kiss.'

His mouth closed over hers and his tongue flicked and
darted against her lips until they parted and their tongues
mingled, tentatively at first then passionately in breathless communion.

Madeleine's hands crept up round Stewart's neck, her
fingers riffled through his thick, silky hair and her
thumbs rubbed at the lobes and rims of his ears.

Their bodies and mouths remained locked together until the insistent buzzing of his mobile, lying on the table,
shredded the silence.

Stewart gave a great, heaving groan and pulled his
mouth from hers. 'Must answer…' He took several deep,
noisy breaths, then kissed her lips softly and just as
gently pushed her away. His eyes were dark, almost
black. He smiled ruefully and picked up the receiver.
'Dr Trellawney,' he announced.

Madeleine could hear a high-pitched gabble in the
background, then Stewart said quietly, 'It sounds like
one of his angina attacks, Doris, but a nasty one. Give
him another tablet—I'll be with you in a few minutes.'
He turned to Madeleine and dropped a kiss on her cheek.

'I'm so sorry, my love, I'll have to dash, and it looks as if I'm going to be some time. May have to get Bernie Black hospitalised. Doris doesn't panic, and it sounds as if he's in a bad way.' He was already striding across the kitchen.

Was he relieved at the interruption? Of course not, how could she think such a thing? He'd simply switched into professional mode to meet an emergency. She'd do the same.

'Can I do anything?' she asked. Like wait up till you get back? she thought, but didn't have the nerve to suggest it.

He shook his head. 'Nothing, thanks. Just get yourself off to bed. One of us may as well get some sleep and be fit for work tomorrow,' he said, blowing her a kiss as he disappeared through the door.

Once in bed, she meant to mull over the ups and downs of the evening, but fell asleep directly her head touched the pillow.

She woke, feeling serenely and intensely happy. Stewart loved her, and any foolish doubts that she'd had about that had disappeared overnight in the mists of sleep. She could look forward to their future together, confident in that love. They had been honest and open with each other—what better start could they have? Given their combined hang-ups, it would take time and patience but they would arrive eventually.

They saw little of each other over the next few days. Phyllis, protesting vigorously, had to go off sick, nearly dead on her feet with a vicious and prolonged attack of migraine. This at once doubled Madeleine's workload.

The health centre was always full and, although agency doctors were engaged to cover from midnight each night, Alison and Stewart were still working flat out. The throat bug was tailing off as mysteriously as it had started, but other winter ills were waiting in the wings to take over, stretching each day to its limits. Stewart continued to do the late evening calls and Madeleine continued to provide him with the occasional meal.

It was the least she could do, she reasoned, since she'd been instrumental in depriving him of his cook in the first place. There was a grain of truth in that, she acknowledged wryly, but in her heart she knew that she would have found another reason to see something of him if that excuse had not been so readily to hand.

The chances of them getting off duty together was presently remote, and their fleeting exchanges on duty were frustrating, to say the least. There was simply no time or opportunity to have a personal conversation, surrounded as they were by other people, so her visits to The Old House, on her errands of mercy, were especially fulfilling.

Something held them back from being as intimate as they had been on that first evening. Perhaps the knowledge that they might be disturbed by the phone inhibited them or perhaps they were each protective of the other's vulnerability and the need to build a solid base for their relationship. But simply to be alone together was something to be treasured.

'This is getting to be a habit, though a nice one,' said Stewart, greeting her with a beaming smile on one occasion when she arrived on his doorstep with a laden tray. 'People will talk.'

She beamed back at him. 'Since they already do,' she said with a chuckle as she followed him through to the now familiar kitchen, 'we have nothing to lose—our reputations are already in tatters. Let's give them something to get their teeth into.'

His eyes gleamed. 'So you're not going to whizz off, like you did last night, and leave me to eat in solitary splendour?'

Maddy shook her head. 'Last night I thought you needed some space after a particularly hectic day. You were very late, getting back, and looked fraught and more than usually tired.'

'I nearly lost a baby with epilepsy. He had a grand mal and was unconscious for forty minutes. It was touch and go at one point while we were waiting for the ambulance to arrive. I know it was late when I got home, but I'd hoped you'd stay and talk. I could have done with your company.'

'Then, for heaven's sake, why didn't you say so?'

He pulled a sad clown's face, his wide mouth turned down at the corners. 'Because, my love, I'm so afraid of taking advantage of that generous nature of yours...'

'And supposing,' Madeleine said softly, her tiger eyes, very bright, fixed on his, 'I *want* you to take advantage of me, give or take my generous nature?'

Stewart drew in a deep, long breath, the pupils of his luminous, pearl grey eyes darkening as they looked into hers. They were standing a couple of feet apart. He reached out, drew her to him and hugged her so tightly she could scarcely breathe, one hand pressing her head against his chest.

Madeleine could hear—feel—his heartbeats, strong and rhythmic, thundering beneath her ear and making her tremble. It was loving and sexy, reassuring and comforting—all that she could wish for, rolled into one. Her lifeline to happiness.

His voice rumbled up from deep in his diaphragm.

'Maddy, more than anything in the world I want to leap into bed with you, make love to you, but I *can't*.'

For a moment she was frozen, unable to comprehend what he was saying. His heart still beat vibrantly beneath her ear. She jerked her head away from his chest, forcing his hand away. 'What do you mean—*can't*?'

'Because I don't want to hurt you. We're neither of us into casual sex without some sort of commitment to a future together. And I can't accept that commitment yet, Maddy, not with my sort of record of marital failure and the reason for it. Being a workaholic can be just as damaging to a relationship as any other addiction. We agreed on friendship, time to get to know each other, remember? Let's stick to that for the moment.'

He made it sound so reasonable, so sensible, she could have thrown something at him.

She said sharply, 'Of course I remember, but does our friendship have to be a sex-free zone? Two consenting adults, friends—I'd hardly call that casual sex. Or are you saying no sex before marriage or...' She frowned, suddenly recalling what he'd said about his sex life diminishing when he was married. Perhaps sex was simply not very important to him, work or no work! If he'd been celibate since his wife died... Her thoughts trailed off into nothingness.

She might as well have spoken those thoughts aloud for, after a moment's silence, Stewart said in a dry, almost amused tone, 'No, I don't have a sex-drive problem—take my word for it. In fact, for a few months after my wife died I went mad for a bit, lived it up rather too well—rebound stuff, I suppose.'

The bleak look was back in his eyes.

'But sex did at one time take second place to work and, as you know, it happened to be at a crucial time in my marriage. And the possibility that it might happen again scares the life out of me because, like it or not, work *is* important to me.' His voice was suddenly harsh, rasping. 'So, you see, Maddy, no way can I let you make any sort of commitment to me until you know me better and I'm more sure of myself—life's too short for you to make that sort of mistake. It's friendship or nothing.'

'It didn't seem much like just friendship a few nights ago. If it hadn't been for that call-out…'

'I know. If it hadn't been for that we'd have ended up in bed together, and don't think I didn't want to.'

'We still could, Stewart.' She knew that her eyes were almost pleading with him.

He shook his head.

Her eyes still pleaded. Had she no pride where he was concerned? Her still, small voice, said *no* loudly and clearly. Well, he might be uncertain about their future together, but she wasn't. All she had to do was be patient and convince him that their love was strong enough to squash the demons of the past. Right, so get on with it.

'So it's friendship or nothing?' She made her voice bright and cheerful.

Expressions of relief and surprise flitted across his face. He'd obviously expected further argument. 'Yes,' he said softly, 'for the time being.'

Madeleine produced a brilliant smile. If I don't smile, she thought, I will burst into tears. 'I'll take it,' she said. She offered a hand. 'Shall we shake on it?'

Stewart went along with the charade. Perhaps he, too, felt like weeping. He took her hand and held it gently. 'Let's seal it with a kiss rather than a handshake,' he said, as he raised it to his lips. 'To friendship.'

'And may it be short and fruitful,' murmured Madeleine, *sotto voce*.

*   *   *

'Thank the Lord,' said Alison the following afternoon as she and Madeleine were clearing up after another hectic asthma clinic, 'that I've got a doting mum who lives nearby and is keeping Roger and me fed during this emergency. I feel sorry for Stewart, having to fend for himself.' She grinned at Madeleine. 'Or has gossip got it right—have you taken to feeding the brute?'

Madeleine found herself blushing, but shrugged and laughed. 'I've taken him an occasional meal,' she said. 'That's about it.'

Alison's grin widened. 'Do you know that some of the locals are calling you "the practice wife"?'

Madeleine said sharply, 'You mean the old witch and her jolly band of back-stabbers?'

Alison shook her head. 'Not that lot. It's being said with affection and, for what it's worth, I think it's rather nice. Stewart's been a changed man since you joined the practice. The old stiffly reserved, hands-off man has vanished, and you know how I've felt about you two right from the beginning. I just can't wait for the practice, or should I say *practice* wife, to become the real thing.'

'You might have a long wait,' replied Madeleine quietly, wondering for a moment whether to confide in her but squashing the idea almost at once.

'No, I don't think so,' said Alison with conviction. 'I'm a bit fey, you know, like most Celts, and I'd say the vibes are right for you right now.'

Madeleine pulled a face and muttered, 'If only.'

'Have faith, my child,' said Alison, with a laugh. 'My instincts are seldom wrong.'

Making her way back to the treatment room, Madeleine couldn't get the phrase 'the practice wife' out of her head.

Did Stewart know that some of the villagers were calling her that? Probably not. When he found out would he mind? She was surprised and touched that it had been, according to Alison, invented by well-wishers in the village and not by the vicious Mrs Gumbrill. Though its sentiment couldn't be mistaken, it underlined the fact that they were constantly in the public eye and that certain things were expected of them.

Her cheeks went hot and cold at the thought and her heart knocked painfully against her ribs. Last night he'd cheerfully accepted that their characters were past redemption, but would he mind that particular label being attached to her, the implication being obvious? Unless, of course, he didn't know, and didn't find out!

Don't be ridiculous, she told herself crossly. If he doesn't already know he will find out—that's the penalty of living in a goldfish bowl.

CHAPTER ELEVEN

IF STEWART knew that Madeleine had been designated 'the practice wife' he kept his own counsel over the hectic, tiring days that followed. Madeleine, seeing him become more hollow-eyed and gaunt, continued to provide him with meals most nights. It was still the most practical way she could relieve the pressure on him, and he clearly appreciated not only the food but her presence.

That he enjoyed having her with him was reassuring, but didn't stop her spirits from flagging. Hard work she could cope with, but the realisation that she was living a farce, pretending just friendship when she wanted so much more, was slowly eating her heart out. How much longer could she keep up this pretence of friendship only?

She wanted Stewart's love, ached with a dull, physical ache in her loins to have his arms round her. She found herself fantasising, sometimes dreaming, of him making passionate, erotic love to her. Occasionally it was so erotic that she woke to find herself sweating and throbbing, her heart pounding painfully in her breast, and hugged herself for warmth and comfort.

Restless and unhappy, she would lie awake, wondering how she could resolve the situation—break through this awful barrier that Stewart's guilt had erected between them, convince him that her love was strong enough to accept what he had to offer and that she was ready and willing to share him with his work.

She always ended up comforting herself with the thought that when Mike returned their tiredness would vanish and they would be able to talk and think clearly. It became like a talisman, a mantra to be chanted...when Mike returns all will be well.

Quite how she didn't know. His return would at one fell stroke relieve the workload, but she was well aware that it wouldn't of itself solve her and Stewart's particular problem. That was something they had to work out for themselves.

Mike returned on a cold and misty February morning.

'Hi, everyone,' he sang out in ringing tones as he bounced into Reception.

Phyllis, Madeleine, Stewart and Alison, all sorting out their lists at the desk, turned as one at the sound of his voice. They were expecting him, yet they all stared for a moment as if he were a stranger from outer space, before mumbling greetings. It was Phyllis who put their combined feelings into words.

'My goodness, you're a sight for sore eyes, Mike,' she said wryly.

He was. Bronzed, his fair hair bleached almost white after his sailing holiday, he brought with him a taste of the sun and fresh sea breezes. But it was his energy that most marked him out. It positively sizzled—he had it, and they didn't. It was as simple as that, and they were all aware of it. He had been away only a fortnight, but it might have been months.

Stewart, who had momentarily seemed as stunned as the rest of them, stepped forward and shook his hand. 'Welcome back, Mike. It *is* good to see you.'

Alison kissed him on the cheek. 'You don't know how good,' she said fervently.

Madeleine and Phyllis each kissed him and gave him a hug.

He twitched his eyebrows. 'Nice,' he said. He leaned

across the counter. 'And what about you ladies?' He offered his cheek to the two receptionists, who pecked at it rather self-consciously.

He grinned round at everyone. 'Well, a welcome I expected, but nothing quite like this,' he said. 'Do I detect a note of relief all round at the return of the prodigal?'

Stewart smiled. 'You could say that.' He glanced at his watch. 'No time to explain now, but let's meet over coffee and I'll put you in the picture. It's been a bit hairy while you were away. Right now we'd all better get cracking before the madding crowd descends upon us.'

'Well, fear not, folks, I'm fighting fit and raring to go,' said Mike, as he picked up a stack of patients' records from the counter.

This was Mike at his willing best. Looking at his boyishly handsome, cheerful face and twinkling blue eyes, Madeleine felt that the pressure was already easing, and when she glanced at the others she could see the same expression of relief on their faces. Life could begin to get back to something like normal.

She met Stewart's eyes, and saw relief mirrored there, too. They exchanged secret smiles.

It was just before one when Stewart rang Madeleine in the treatment room.

'I badly need some fresh air, exercise…and you, Maddy.' There seemed to be a note almost of urgent desperation in his voice. 'Get changed, ready to walk. We'll pick up a pasty from the bakery and go up on the moors for an hour or so. I haven't got a surgery till four and the paperwork can wait. Please try to fix something with Phyllis.'

Madeleine caught her breath. It was unbelievable, he was actually prepared to shelve the mountain of paperwork which had amassed during the crisis for a few hours with her. Her heart knocked against her ribs and her stomach churned. Was he trying to tell her something, was this some sort of breakthrough? Or had she imagined the urgency in his voice? Did he only need fresh air and exercise and some company?

Don't get your hopes up, she warned herself.

'I'll see what I can do,' she said evenly. 'I'll ring you back after I've spoken to Phyll.'

'Of course you must go,' said Phyllis. 'Do you both the world of good. You've hardly been out of the place for weeks.' She winked. 'Go and do a Cathy and Heathcliff up on the wind-swept moors. I'll manage. After all, I owe you—you held the fort when I had my migraine.'

It was a brilliant afternoon, and the sun shone out of an almost clear sky of pale winter blue.

'What a pity—there's no wind,' exclaimed Madeleine, as they reached the top of the twisting track out of the village and paused to look out across the undulating moorland.

Stewart took her hand and swung it between them. It was such a small thing, yet she trembled with pleasure—it felt so right, having her hand in his. It occurred to her that they had never been out walking together.

He raised his eyebrows. 'Why the need for a wind?' he asked.

She threw back her head and laughed. She felt incredibly light-hearted. 'Phyllis thinks it's a must so that we can do a Cathy and Heathcliff, running headlong into each other's arms—you know, *Wuthering Heights*.'

'Phyllis is an incurable romantic, bless her heart,' he said. 'But, be patient, there'll be at least a stiff breeze when we get up there.' He pointed into the distance to some ruins on top of a craggy outcrop of rock, stark and forbidding against the blue sky. 'It was a castle of sorts, built by a power-mad tin-mine owner in the middle of the last century so that he could look out over the mines and land that he owned. Sadly, all that remain now are a few broken-down workings of his one-time empire.'

'It looks quite a climb to the top. Is it far?'

'About a mile as the crow flies, but further on foot because the path twists and turns and is quite steep in places. It's not really that high, just looks it on account of the flattish moorland that surrounds it, but once you reach the top you can see for miles right to the coast. Take us a bit over half an hour to get there.'

'Can we eat before we start climbing? I'm starving.'

He squeezed her hand. 'Well, that is good news. You've not been eating much lately, at least not when we were supposed to be sharing one of your delicious suppers. Half the time you've just been pushing the food around on your plate. Must be the fresh air.' He breathed in a great lungful.

Madeleine felt the colour come and go in her cheeks. She wanted to say, Fresh air be damned. It's because I'm here with you and there's something different about you today. I'm happy and being happy makes me hungry, but instead she murmured, 'I didn't think you'd noticed. You've been so tired these last few days.'

Stewart lifted her chin and looked into her eyes. 'I notice everything about you, Maddy,' he said in his quiet, deep voice. He bent his head and kissed her gently on her lips. 'Come on, we'll sit over there and have our lunch.' He pointed to a cluster of rocks a hundred yards away.

They sat down with their backs against the smooth, rounded boulders. He handed her a fragrant, still-warm pasty in a paper bag. 'Tuck in, let me see you eat.' His eyes, bright and luminous, reflecting some of the blue of the sky, met hers.

Madeleine shifted her gaze down to the bag she was holding, carefully peeled back the edges of the paper and took a huge bite out of the pasty. 'Mmm, scrumptious,' she mumbled, puffing out a few flakes of pastry.

Stewart beamed at her. 'Well done,' he said, as if she'd performed some clever magic trick. He peeled back the paper from his own pasty and bit into it with his large, white, even teeth.

With shoulders touching and tinglingly aware of each other's closeness, their faces turned to the sun and bathed in its mild warmth. Revelling in the peace and quiet that surrounded them, they munched away in silence. They finished eating at the same moment.

'A dead heat,' said Stewart. He took Madeleine's empty bag from her, screwed it up and put it into the pocket of his waxed jacket. With a long finger he brushed a crumb from her lips. 'We must have looked like two contented cows, chewing the cud,' he murmured.

His eyes devoured her, sweeping over her semi-recumbent form from head to toe and back again, before coming to rest on her mouth. He leaned towards her, his mouth hovering above hers. 'Oh, Maddy,' he whispered against her lips. His arms went round her.

'Stewart…'

Their mouths and tongues met and melded in one long, tender, passionate, sexy, breathless kiss. Their hands moved urgently, tugging at clothing—smoothing, squeezing, stroking—until suddenly Stewart broke away. He took a long, shuddering breath. 'I don't want to stop,' he said hoarsely, 'but if we're to climb up to the castle we'd better get on with it.'

'Do we have to?' Maddy whispered.

His mouth quirked into a lopsided smile. 'Yes,' he said, 'for this is neither the time nor place for what I have in mind.'

He stood up and offered his hand. Madeleine took it and he hauled her to her feet.

Madeleine stared at him, as if she were seeing him for the first time. Her heart seemed to stand still, though her pulses raced, and her breathing was fast and shallow. 'What *do* you have in mind?' she whispered.

'I'll tell you when we get to the top.' He was suddenly very brisk. 'Come on, Maddy, let's do what we came out to do and walk.' He took her hand and started off so briskly that Madeleine had to run to keep up with him.

'Hey,' she said breathlessly, 'slow down—you're going like a bat out of hell.'

'Sorry.' He slanted her a brief smile and slowed down a little, but she still had to walk very fast to keep up with him.

He seemed disinclined to talk but she didn't mind, partly because she was too breathless to talk and partly because she wanted to think. Not that her thoughts made much sense. They were mostly a series of staccato unanswerable questions. Why had he suddenly decided on the walk? What was it that he had to tell her? Dared she hope it was something that was going to change their whole future? Had he had a change of heart—was that what that spectacular kiss had meant? She took a deep, shuddering breath and stumbled.

Stewart transferred his grip to her elbow. 'You all right, Maddy?'

She nodded.

'Not far now.'

She looked around her in surprise. They were within a few hundred yards of the foot of the rocky outcrop.

Deep in thought, she'd hardly noticed the distance they'd covered.

Stewart was looking toward the outcrop, too, not at the summit but at something moving near the foot.

Madeleine said, 'It's a boy, running like the wind.'

They saw the boy change direction and head toward them.

Stewart frowned. 'I think something's up.' He stepped forward as the boy threw himself at him, gulping in great mouthfuls of air and trying to speak.

'It's all right, old son,' Stewart said, gripping the boy's shoulders, 'take your time. It's Bobby Prendergast, isn't it?'

'Yes,' gasped the boy.

'OK, Bobby, tell me what's happened.'

The boy stuck out a shaky arm and pointed toward the crag. 'It's Terry, me mate,' he said in a shrill, trembling voice. 'He's fallen down a hole up there.'

'Do you mean a mine shaft?'

'Yes, it's near the top.'

'Have you spoken to him?'

'No. He just lies there. He won't answer me and he's too deep down to reach.'

'Right, Bobby. We'll look after Terry. You go to the surgery, tell them *I* sent you and it's urgent. Explain what's happened. You be ready to guide them back so that they don't miss us. They'll know what to do about organising help. Go as quickly as you can, but take care. You've done brilliantly so far. Can you manage that?'

Bobby nodded and took off for the village while Stewart and Madeleine made for the crag at a fast jog.

The shaft was a bit to the side of the track and easily missable. It was just possible to make out the shapes of low, broken-down walls and unidentifiable rusting ironwork, half-smothered by weeds and brambles. Pushing their way cautiously through the tangle of vegetation, conscious that there was a yawning hole in the ground somewhere in the vicinity, they suddenly came upon a couple of sheets of corrugated iron bolted to a wooden frame—clearly a cover of some sort.

The ground around it had recently been disturbed and it had been shifted partly to one side, exposing a wedge of blackness beneath.

Motioning Maddy to remain where she was, Stewart moved still more cautiously forward and lay flat to peer through the aperture. 'Terry's there all right, but I can only just make him out. Go carefully round the other side and help me shift this right back to let in more light.' His voice was crisp and matter-of-fact, yet reassuringly unhurried.

Maddy did as he instructed and together they lifted and dragged the cover clear. They both knelt to peer into the hole.

The boy was lying pale and still about twelve feet down. He was sprawled on a loose, flimsy, criss-cross raft of timbers that had evidently jammed across the shaft. Rusting bolt-heads were visible, lining the walls from where the shoring timbers had torn free from the sides.

Their eyes met across the void, holding the same question. Was the boy dead or just unconscious?

Suddenly, without warning, the rough raft of timber moved and tilted slightly.

They both breathed in sharply and Stewart muttered, 'Hell,' and then called softly, 'Terry, can you hear me? Answer me if you can but don't move suddenly.'

There was no answer and the boy's eyes remained closed, but he did move or rather twitched.

At least he's alive, thought Maddy. 'Do you think he's coming round?' she whispered.

'Possibly, but we've got to get down to him, make sure he doesn't move violently, or that lot's going to collapse.' He stood. 'What we need is a chain or rope... There must be something lying around.' He began to search through the undergrowth, wrenching apart brambles and ignoring the thorns.

Maddy worked feverishly beside him, not noticing the scratches to her hands. A chain—rope. He meant to lower himself into the shaft. He couldn't. Wasn't possible, too dangerous. Her stomach heaved.

'Will this do?' She struggled to wrest a heavy coil of rusting, small-link chain from a patch of weeds in which it was embedded.

Stewart hauled it free and uncoiled it. 'Yes. I'll tie it round me, fix the other end to something...' They looked around at the weeds and brambles.

'There isn't anything,' said Maddy. 'I'm lighter, I'll go down. You can lower me, act as anchor man.'

Stewart stared at her, aghast. 'No. I won't let you...too dangerous.'

She kept her voice steady. 'I have to, there's no other option. We can't stand around while that child...'

He said grimly. 'You're right—no option.'

He looped the chain under her arms and tied it across her chest above her breasts. 'Won't be comfortable but we haven't time to make up a fancy harness.' He gave her a little slack, looped the other end of the chain over his arm, braced his legs and said, 'Ready—and, for God's sake, my darling, please take care, no heroics.'

For a fraction of a second his eyes met hers, pleading, loving, fearful.

Maddy fought not to let him see how scared she was, and nodded. 'I will,' she promised.

She sat, swung her legs over the edge, twisted around so that she faced the side of the shaft and began her descent. The chain bit into the flesh under her arms. Stewart, keeping it taut, paid it out slowly as she groped for toe- and finger-holds. The downward journey seemed endless.

'You're nearly there—watch your feet,' Stewart called suddenly.

She looked down cautiously, and carefully placed her feet against the beam ends of the raft where they were wedged against the side of the shaft.

'OK, give me some slack,' she gasped.

Stewart paid out a bit more chain and she was able to bend over the boy's still form.

She lifted his eyelids and examined the pupils—they looked normal, even. It was a good sign. With infinite care, she felt around the back of his head. There was a small lump near the crown, but no blood. She ran her fingers down his neck and back as far as she could reach, then gently down his arms and legs. She took his pulse. It was a bit fast but strong and regular, his respirations were good and there was no sign of internal bleeding.

'I can't find anything wrong,' she called up to Stewart, 'except that he's concussed, but only lightly I think.'

At that moment Terry stirred again. One of the beams under him dropped a few inches. Rigid with fear, Maddy held her breath as debris pattered away into the dark depths below them.

'Watch out!' Stewart bellowed.

Instinct and a rush of adrenaline gave her the strength to haul up the boy's inert form and hug him to her as, with a grinding crash, the jumble of beams fell away from under them. She felt her foot-holds vanish and she swung free like a pendulum over the abyss. Suddenly and agonisingly, all her weight and Terry's was being supported by the loop of chain, biting into her chest.

Then they were rising foot by slow foot. She could

hear Stewart grunting and panting with the effort of lifting them both. She prayed that his strength wouldn't fail. All she could do was cling desperately to Terry's limp form to stop him slipping out of her arms. Her head and shoulders rose above the lip of the shaft. Stewart edged along until his feet were braced on either side of the corner and he pulled again, lifting them another foot. With a massive heave she humped the boy onto solid ground.

Stewart, breathing harshly, reached down, grasped the chain loop round her chest and hauled her clear of the shaft. They both collapsed onto their knees, trembling from their exertions. With shaking hands he tried to loosen the knotted chain about her chest. It hurt like hell. She saw that his hands were streaked with rust and blood. 'Leave it, leave it, I'm all right,' she gasped. 'Check the boy.'

Slowly he crawled over to Terry on hands and knees, dragged him away from the edge of the shaft and examined him quickly with his bloody hands. He confirmed what Maddy had said. There were no obvious signs of broken bones or internal bleeding, and pulse and respirations were a little fast but strong and even. The boy's pupils showed no sign of deep unconsciousness, but were equal in size and normal-looking. Amazingly it seemed that he had escaped serious injuries.

Stewart rolled him into the recovery position and was just about to cover him with his jacket when Terry opened his eyes and stared at him.

Stewart gave him a moment to focus, then said, 'Terry, do you know who I am?'

There was a moment's pause then he mumbled, 'You're our doctor.'

'You've had a bit of an accident but you're safe now. How do you feel?'

'OK, I think. Head aches a bit.'

'Not surprising, you've had a bump. Just lie still, old chap. Someone will be coming to fetch us in a minute.'

'OK.' Terry closed his eyes.

Stewart returned to Madeleine's side. 'He's come round,' he said in answer to her unspoken question, 'and he's fine. Amazing, no sign of anything serious, as far as I can see.'

'Thank goodness,' she said fervently.

He saw that she was still struggling to undo the chain around her chest, wincing as she did so. 'Here, let me,' he said softly. This time his hands weren't shaking. His fingers still seemed to be working, she noticed. The blood was on his palms. He freed the rusty links. 'You're going to have one hell of a bruise,' he said as he slipped it off, revealing a rusty indent in her tracksuit top where it had bitten into the material.

Tentatively she brushed at the rust marks. 'Doesn't matter.' Relief that the worst was over flooded through her. The boy was safe, she and Stewart were safe. What were a few cuts and bruises? 'I'll heal.' She looked him straight in the eye. 'People *do*, you know—they heal from all sorts of wounds.'

'Indeed they do.' Gently he put an arm round her shoulder and cradled her head against his chest. It was still there a little later when they heard the first of the rescue convoy, roaring up to the base of the crag.

The church clock struck eight as Stewart rang Madeleine's kitchen doorbell. He'd come as promised.

'I shall bring *you* supper tonight,' he'd said when they'd parted at the end of the long, traumatic afternoon. 'Mike's doing the evening calls.'

'But you can't—your poor hands.'

'Quite capable of conjuring up something to eat.'

He'd cupped her face with his damaged hands. 'My dear, brave, darling Maddy, go and soak in a long, hot bath, anoint yourself with healing oils and change into something comfortable,' he'd instructed.

He'd kissed her tenderly on the mouth as they'd stood at the foot of the winding staircase. His eyes had twinkled, gobbled her up. There had been no sign of the overworked doctor or the man exhausted with the gigantic effort of hauling two people to safety. He had been like a man reborn. Like a man in love...

Déjà vu. A lifetime ago there'd been another night as the church had struck and Stewart had stood on her doorstep...

Her heart tumbled like a wild thing in her bruised chest. Maddy opened the door wide and he stepped into the kitchen. He kissed her on the cheek and thrust a carrier bag under her nose. 'Smell that,' he said. 'Supper, as promised.'

She sniffed, and the delicious aroma of fish and chips and vinegar wafted up from the bag. It was reassuringly homely, down-to-earth. 'That's cheating.' She chuckled. 'You didn't labour over a hot stove.'

He put the bag down and held up his bandaged hands. 'Excuse!' he said, his eyes bright with laughter. 'Now, let's eat while it's hot.'

They took their plates through to the sitting room.

'By the way,' Stewart said, as they began to eat slowly and leisurely, conscious of the whole evening stretching before them, 'I had a visit from Mrs Gumbrill just before I left.'

Maddy gaped at him. 'That old witch—why? What sort of venom is she dripping this time?'

Stewart grinned and popped a chip into her open mouth. 'Actually, she came to thank us.'

She nearly choked on her chip. 'Thank *us*... What do you mean?'

'For rescuing young Terry—he's her grandson, didn't you know?'

Maddy shook her head, her eyes wide with astonishment. 'I'd no idea... Thank us! Lord, that must have hurt her.'

'As a matter of fact, she was very dignified about it, very generous. Was particularly concerned to know how you're doing. Somehow I don't think there'll be any more nasty rumours circulating. The war's over, Maddy.'

'Well, there's a thought—flavour of the month rather than scarlet woman.'

'Talking of scarlet,' he said softly, 'I bet you've got some highly coloured bruising where that chain bit into you. What did Alison think of it?'

'Said I got away with it lightly, considering. Escaped first-degree burns on account of my thick tracksuit. She prescribed hamamelis gel to bring out the bruising.'

Their eyes locked across the table, pearl grey fusing with tawny and flashing all sorts of vibes and messages back and forth.

Maddy held her breath, felt the blood steal up into her cheeks and willed the moment to go on and on for ever and ever...

Stewart's voice, rumbling, husky, came from a long way off. 'I can prescribe something better—an old-fashioned treatment for cuts and bruises much more efficient than unguents and gels.'

As if in a trance, her lips moved. 'What is it...this treatment?'

He stood and moved around the table, bending over her and drawing her to her feet. In one fluid, easy movement he swept her up into his arms, cradling her with infinite gentleness so as not to crush her injured chest. He carried her across the room through the door into her bedroom.

'I can kiss them better,' he said, 'like this.' He kissed her nose. 'Or this.' His lips brushed hers, then travelled down her neck to the hollow in her throat, teasing, tormenting with little licking kisses, then moved back up again. 'That,' he murmured against her mouth, 'is just a sample.' His pupils were huge, dark, hungry, loving.

Maddy gazed into them and felt she was drowning in them, sinking down, down into their tender, grey velvety depths. She whispered, 'No one's ever kissed me better before.'

'Then it's high time someone did.'

'Make love to me, Stewart,' she begged, 'please.'

He lowered her onto the bed. She wouldn't let him straighten, but put her arms round his neck, imprisoning him then pulling him down beside her.

He turned to look at her. 'You're sure about this? You know it means taking me on, bag and baggage?'

'I've been sure for weeks,' she said. 'What about you? You're the one who's doubted.'

'Not any more, my love. That's what I planned to tell you this afternoon—that the healing process has worked. I'm a well man.' He lifted his head and leaned on his elbow, looking down at her. 'I was going to ask you to marry me…'

'*Were* going to?'

'*Am* asking you. Will you marry me, Maddy?'

'Yes. Will you make love to me, Stewart?'

His eyes gleamed wickedly and his lovely, sexy mouth curved into a wide smile. 'Nothing,' he murmured, 'is going to stop me.' Slowly he began unfastening the buttons of her velvet leisure suit. 'And I shall start, as promised, by kissing your bruises better…'

And with infinite, sensual tenderness he did.

CHAPTER TWELVE

'THE wedding,' Maddy told Fee and Naomi when she phoned with her news a few days later, 'is to be on May the first.'

'May Day,' breathed Naomi. 'How rustic and romantic—all those frolicking nymphs and shepherds and cider and things.'

Madeleine spluttered. 'My dear Naomi, you've got a weird idea of the countryside *circa* the nineteen-nineties, city girl that you are. And it'll be champagne, vintage stuff... And, please, I want you both to be bridesmaids or maids of honour or whatever.'

Fee wailed, 'But I'll be all busty and milky...'

'And a picture of perfect motherhood. We had thought of March or early April, but decided that your little orthopod might put in an early or late appearance so we plumped for May.'

'Have you thought about dresses?' asked Naomi, going directly to the important issue, as she saw it.

'Hardly, hasn't been time, but what about something Empire-ish, vaguely Austen? Think about it, just keep me in the picture. By the way, another favour—Fee, do you think your senior orthopod would give me away?'

'He'll jump at the chance. You know my Tim—it bothers him that you're the only one of us still footloose and fancy-free. You know how he likes everything neat and tidy in their right pigeonholes, as in Theatre at the start of an op.'

Madeleine laughed. 'Well, you can assure him that I'm no longer footloose, and have no wish to be fancy-free,' she said firmly. 'I can't wait to be pigeonholed as a married woman.'

A few days before the wedding Stewart's parents arrived. They had torn themselves away from their mission hospital to be with him. From the word go they had warmed to Madeleine and she to them.

Madeleine found it easy to like them. Dr Trellawney senior was simply an older, grey-haired version of Stewart, and Moira Trellawney reminded her of her foster mum, Rose. Like her, she was tough, gentle, down-to-earth and utterly reliable, and the fact that they would be living far apart in the forseeable future wouldn't stop them becoming friends, good friends. She would be a mother-in-law in a million.

The horse-drawn carriage, which Stewart had arranged as a surprise, drew up in front of the lych-gate at the foot of the path up to the church. This particular May Day, thought Madeleine as Tim handed her out of the elegant vehicle, was all that the poets crack it up to be. A blue and gold day, with the birds singing like crazy and bees buzzing around the lichen-covered, ancient gravestones.

There was a sigh of satisfaction from the little knot of bystanders, waiting at the gate as she alighted. She blushed faintly. She knew she looked good—'stunning', according to Tim. She made an exquisite, radiant bride in gold-tinted oyster satin and matching short tulle veil, anchored by a coronet of deep gold roses to complement her bouquet.

She was a golden bride, from her tawny hair, brushed to a gleaming cap, to the toes of her satin pumps. She floated up the aisle on Tim's arm, followed by Fee and

Naomi—a striking contrast in their Empire-line dark blue silk gowns.

A sea of familiar faces turned to admire Maddy as she sailed by but she only had eyes for Stewart, at the altar beside Mike, watching her approach with a tender, loving smile on his face. He took her hand as she arrived beside him and pressed it gently.

'You look beautiful,' he breathed, his pearl-grey eyes luminous with love.

The organ stopped, the congregation sat, the service began...

The words of the old service that they'd chosen tumbled around her.

'If there is anyone...?'

'Do you take this man...?'

She, herself, saying firmly, 'I do.'

Stewart sliding the wide band of gold on her finger.

Her feeling of intense, all-embracing happiness.

The vicar said, 'You are now man and wife—you may kiss the bride.'

Stewart bent his head—and a bleeper sounded. 'Thank God that's for Alison, she's on call,' he murmured, kissing Maddy very thoroughly.

The vicar coughed. 'If you'll just come this way.'

Madeleine had an unholy desire to giggle as they followed him into the vestry, but squashed it. Hysteria! She was ludicrously happy.

In a dream, she signed the register—'Madeleine Trellawney'. There were kisses and congratulations all round.

They left the vestry, the organ triumphantly ringing out the first quivering notes of the 'Trumpet Voluntary'. Six-week-old James—Fee's little orthopod—let out a protesting wail. A ripple of amusement ran round the congregation.

Stewart grinned. 'Don't think he approves of our choice of music,' he said as he and Madeleine, arm in arm, made their way down the aisle.

'Well, at least it proves that my godson-to-be has a good pair of lungs on him,' said Madeleine, beaming at all the smiling faces turned toward them.

Half the village seemed to be there, patients who had been her supporters from the beginning and to her surprise, some who hadn't—Mrs Gumbrill prominent among them.

Stewart had noticed her too. His eyes twinkled. 'Told you the war was well and truly over,' he murmured, squeezing Madeleine's arm tucked securely into his.

They stood for a moment alone in the porch. He bent and kissed her swiftly. 'And how does it feel to be Mrs Trellawney, the real thing and not the ''practice'' wife?'

'Complete!' she said firmly.

CHRISTMAS

Affairs

MORE THAN JUST KISSES UNDER THE MISTLETOE...

Enjoy three sparkling seasonal romances by your
favourite authors from

MILLS & BOON®
Presents™

HELEN BIANCHIN
For Anique, the season of goodwill has become...
The Seduction Season

SANDRA MARTON
Can Santa weave a spot of Christmas magic for Nick
and Holly in... *A Miracle on Christmas Eve?*

SHARON KENDRICK
Will Aleck and Clemmie have a... *Yuletide Reunion?*

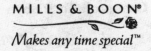

MILLS & BOON®
Makes any time special™

Available from 6th November 1998

MILLS & BOON®

Next Month's Romance Titles

♡

Each month you can choose from a wide variety of romance novels from Mills & Boon®. Below are the new titles to look out for next month from the Presents™ and Enchanted™ series.

Presents™

PACIFIC HEAT	Anne Mather
THE BRIDAL BED	Helen Bianchin
THE YULETIDE CHILD	Charlotte Lamb
MISTLETOE MISTRESS	Helen Brooks
A CHRISTMAS SEDUCTION	Amanda Browning
THE THIRTY-DAY SEDUCTION	Kay Thorpe
FIANCÉE BY MISTAKE	Kate Walker
A NICE GIRL LIKE YOU	Alexandra Sellers

Enchanted™

FIANCÉ FOR CHRISTMAS	Catherine George
THE HUSBAND PROJECT	Leigh Michaels
COMING HOME FOR CHRISTMAS	Laura Martin
THE BACHELOR AND THE BABIES	Heather MacAllister
THE NUTCRACKER PRINCE	Rebecca Winters
FATHER BY MARRIAGE	Suzanne Carey
THE BILLIONAIRE'S BABY CHASE	Valerie Parv
ROMANTICS ANONYMOUS	Lauryn Chandler

On sale from 4th December 1998

H1 9811

Available at most branches of WH Smith, Tesco, Asda, Martins, Borders and all good paperback bookshops